I0627909

AMARI

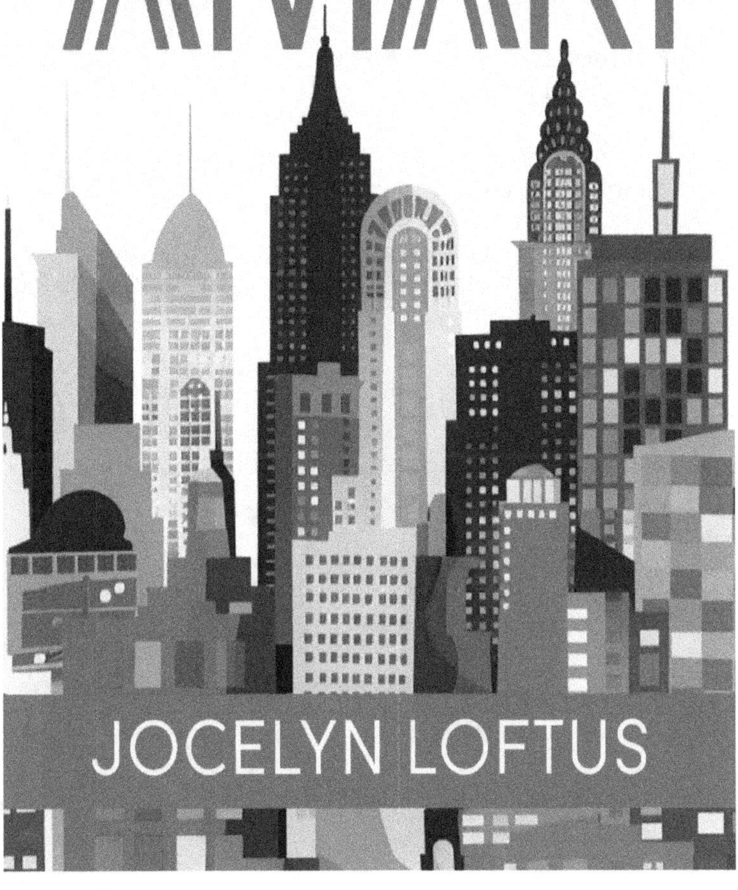

JOCELYN LOFTUS

Copyright © 2024 by **Jocelyn Loftus**

All rights reserved. No portion of this publication may be reproduced, stored in an electronic system, or transmitted in any form by any means, electronic, mechanical, photocopy, recording, or otherwise, without the author's prior permission, except with brief quotations used in literary reviews and specific non-commercial uses permitted by copyright law. For permission requests, please contact the publisher at the website listed below.

This book is a work of fiction. Names, characters, places, and incidents are either the product of the author's imagination or are used fictitiously. Any resemblance to actual persons, living or dead, businesses, companies, events, or locales is entirely coincidental.

For questions and comments about the quality of the book, please contact the publisher at the email address below.

Cover and Interior Layout @ 2024 Harvest Creek Publishing and Design
www.harvestcreek.net e-mail: info@harvestcreek.net

Ordering Information: Special discounts are available on quantity purchases by groups, churches, and other associations. For details, please contact the publisher at the email address listed.

Amari—1st edition.

ISBN: 978-1-961641-15-0

Printed in The United States of America

AMARI

CH/\PTER 1

I WAKE UP TO sweaty palms and heavy breathing. Rubbing the sleep from my eyes, I recall my dream where I was watching the ocean waves skirt the sand on the shore. A storm is brewing far out in the ocean, but I know it won't reach me for several hours.

I want to fall back asleep, feeling the serenity of the ocean and avoiding the big choices ahead of me. Today is the first day of the Evaluation, a five-day test that assesses our physical and mental abilities. This determines if we fall in the Brawn or Brain category. That's what everyone calls them, but their real names are Vigor and Intelligence. These labels determine what our strengths and weaknesses are.

Generally, the Vigor and the Brain don't get along. One considers the other to be stupid, while the other considers one to be weak. It's a mutual feeling. I am one of the few that have friends in both categories. In the grand scheme of things, I don't understand what the big fuss is. We are all just regular people who happen to have different strengths and weaknesses.

In any case, the Evaluation is mandatory for everyone at the age of eighteen. It will tell us which category we fit into. I really don't want to take the Evaluation. It is basically a lengthy test that scrutinizes our flaws and tells us who we are—no personal choice, just orders.

However, there is some beauty within the system. The system ensures that everyone fits in where they are placed, so no one stands out as the weird kid. My greatest fear is that I will end up somewhere I don't like. After all, I don't want to hate the whole "Evaluation" experience and the next few months of my life.

"Breakfast is ready, Kiara! Time to get up!" Mom made cinnamon rolls this morning; the aroma travels to my room from the kitchen. She only makes them on special occasions.

"Coming, Mom!" I jump out of bed and pull on a pair of jeans and a T-shirt. After tying my hair in a ponytail, I gently dab my eyelashes with mascara and brush powder across my face. Before heading downstairs, I take a moment to myself and look in the mirror. I am by no means tall, but I wouldn't call myself short, either. My face is beautifully framed by my auburn hair, causing my blue eyes to stand out. I inherited my mom's features, her dark blue eyes and small, pointed nose.

My brother got Mom's deep brown hair with flecks of blonde. Despite the hair, my brother Jacob resembles my dad. They are both tall and have a lean but muscular build. Many girls think

Jacob is handsome. To me, he looks like my silly little brother. Even though he is two years younger than me, we share an unbreakable bond.

After taking one last look in the mirror, I walk down our dark oak stairwell, hearing the creak of a few boards that need to be replaced. I'm going to miss this place when I leave for training. I grab a cinnamon roll from the center of our table, icing dripping over my fingers. It is still warm from the oven, and steam rises from it as I take a bite.

Mom looks over at me with narrowed eyes. She can always see straight through my attempt at a calm face. I wonder if my nerves are that noticeable.

"Good morning." I wonder what it was like when she took *her* test.

"Good morning, Kiara. Now, I know you might be nervous, but trust me, there is no need because the results you receive do not define you."

Despite having a big bite of cinnamon roll in my mouth, I give her a grateful smile. "Thanks, Mom."

"Plus, the test only shows you what you are best suited for. It's not like your life will completely change after that moment. If you really want to, you can ignore the test and choose where you want to go." She pauses and looks me in the eye. She takes a deep breath and smiles. "Always remember, I love you and know you will do great no matter what." She hugs me and kisses me on the forehead.

"I love you, too, Mom." Anxiety builds up inside of me as I walk out of our front door. Once I hop into my car, butterflies fill my stomach.

As I drive to our testing building, which happens to be our two-story school in the middle of our city, I consider the opportunities awaiting me: an engineer, a businesswoman, a teacher.

When I arrive there, I park my car in the school parking lot. As soon as I slam my car door shut, a female body comes flying at me—Clara. We first met in sixth grade and have not parted since. She is a Brawn, or at least her parents are. My parents are both in Brain. That difference does not separate us, though. Who knows? We might both end up in Brain or Brawn together.

"Are you ready? It's going to be so much fun! I have. . ." she continues to drone on as we walk to the main gym. That is one thing I can always count on Clara for. Her excitement and optimism are evident in everything she does. Today, I wish I had her enthusiasm, but I don't.

Clara and I walk through the gym doors and rush to get good seats in the stands near the front. There is a microphone in the center of the gym. Once everyone is seated and silent, our principal walks out to address us. "Hello, everyone. Welcome to the first day of your five consecutive testing days. Today, I am privileged to invite Ms. Lily Cassini to the stage. She will inform you of the ways in which testing will be performed. Please give her a round of applause."

As she walks up to the microphone, the crowd claps loudly. Then, the applause slowly dies down until there is nothing but silence. Once everyone is quietly looking at her, Ms. Cassini taps the microphone and addresses us.

"Ladies and gentlemen, I am so glad to see you here. Today, you will learn about your future. For the past century, the Evaluation has been a longstanding tradition in our nation. It helps us characterize each one of you, and it allows us to put you in a place where you will flourish and grow in your abilities.

"The test is split into three days, with one day on either end, to explain the procedure and present your results. The first day will contain a printed exam, including concepts and ideas that you have and have not learned. This will test your ability to think and apply your previous knowledge. We are looking for reasoning and awareness. Many jobs, such as doctors, teachers, and scientists, are offered if you excel in this area of testing.

"The second day comprises a series of physical challenges that test your strength and endurance, along with your ability to learn quickly. Performing well on these can lead to a career as a sports player, a farmer, or a builder. The third day will put you inside virtual reality situations. Your choices will tell us how your personality fits in with those around you, along with your virtues and vices. On the last day, your results will be given to you by one of the instructors. Most people excel in one area or the other, and their personality will correspond with their strengths."

Her tone suddenly shifts from her pleasant and carefree tone to a serious one. A grave face replaces her easy smile. "A few people perform above average on both tests. Their personality is confused and obscure. These people are dangerous!"

Ms. Cassini's face and tone switch back to her easy-going, happy self. "But don't worry about that because I can assure you that none of you will be that person. You will most likely follow your parents into an ordinary life in either Vigor or Intelligence.

"This concludes my speech for the day. Thank you for your undivided attention. The instructors, Luke and Lora, will be showing you how the testing will proceed. Boys, go with Luke to the physical test. Girls, follow Lora to the mental test. You are dismissed."

As she walks out, confusion hits the room. The instructors are yelling at their designated followers. Everyone moves in different directions, trying to follow their leader.

Eventually, the confusion subsides, and we are all in our respective groups. Lora leads us to the cafeteria. Instead of lunch tables, there are rows and rows of desks. The room looks odd compared to the everyday hustle of the cafe I'm familiar with. We all gather around her.

"Listen up! My name is Lora. My job today is to explain how the mental testing is to proceed. Any questions before we start?" She pauses for a few seconds.

"Good," she continues. "Since around two hundred seniors are taking the test tomorrow, you will be split into four groups of fifty. Two groups will take the test at a time, one in the cafe and one in the gym. The test takes approximately two hours to complete and contains 100 questions.

"You may be asked anything from 'What is the capital of England?' to 'Which section of your brain controls your decision-making?' You will not know the answer to many of these questions, so try your best to answer them well. These questions are designed to make you think. Once everyone is finished, Ms. Cassini will give another short speech, and you will be released. Any questions?" Her speech sounded like it was memorized.

"How high must you score to be considered outstanding?" asks a short girl from the back of the crowd.

"Ninety percent, or 90 out of 100. Any more questions?" Lora asks.

"Is there any way to perform outstanding on both tests?"

"As Ms. Cassini mentioned earlier, very few people do, but the average person performs close to outstanding on one test and poorly on the other test," Lora responds.

"Will we just have to wait for two hours for the other groups to finish? What are we going to do?" a girl with bright red lipstick and curly blonde hair asks.

"Yes, you will have to wait. You can talk among yourselves when you are on the football field, but you may not discuss the test once you have taken it. No comparing answers or asking questions about the test. Is that all?"

"Why can't we talk about our tests?" the same curly blonde girl asks.

"It's against the rules. No more questions? Okay, then. I'll call Luke and see if he's done with the boys." She walks off about ten feet and calls someone, presumably Luke.

"That was intense," Clara whispers to me, her bright, green eyes round with excitement.

"Yeah. I wonder if the test is really that hard," I reply.

"It will probably be like finals, except you don't know what to study."

"Exactly. Just as hard, but you aren't given anything to study for in advance."

"All right, everyone. Luke is done with the boys. Head on over to the football field. He will be waiting there. Have fun!" Lora smiles and waves us off as we walk out to the football field.

When we reach the field, a boy around the age of twenty, who is standing in the end zone, calls us over. He has dark brown hair with light brown streaks. My heart flutters for a moment. His deep blue eyes catch mine, and he stares at me for a few moments. *This must be Luke.* Confident that he's sizing me up and scrutinizing my flaws, I drop my eyes to the ground.

"Hello, ladies. Are you ready to find out what your future holds in store? Good! The physical segment of the test consists of three parts that occur throughout the day. First, you will learn techniques and apply them. Even if you don't go into physical training, it is still a good idea to learn self-defense. Some of the techniques include knife-throwing, punching, and shooting a gun. The following section, endurance, will take you through a series of workouts. You will run a course full of obstacles and perform a certain number of push-ups and sit-ups.

The third section will be fighting. "Don't worry. You might end up with a couple of bruises, but nothing too serious. This just tests your awareness of difficult situations and how you react to them. The better you perform, the harder we will push you. All two hundred of you will be split up into four groups of fifty: two groups of fifty girls and two groups of fifty boys. Each section takes approximately two hours, and each group will have an off-period to rest. Now, any questions?"

"Will we have to fight you?" the small girl from the back of the crowd asks.

"Yes. You will have to fight me, but I promise I will go easy on you."

"Do we have to do this? What if we want to go into Brain? I don't want to waste a day doing exercises I will never use."

"Even if you don't use these exercises on a daily basis, it will benefit you. Plus, it is required." Luke looks away from the girl who asked that question, a slight look of shock and annoyance on his face. I don't think he expected such an outright question from her.

"Do you have a girlfriend?" the girl with blonde hair and red lipstick asks. Her name is Sarah.

Blushing slightly, Luke is caught off guard. "If there are no more real questions, then you can head back to the gym," he replies, ignoring the last question. With a slight frown, he calls someone and tells them that we are finished.

As a group, we walk back to the gym and listen to Ms. Cassini's speech. She says something about resting and eating well. I don't really listen because all I can think about is the test tomorrow.

CH/\PTER 2

MY ALARM CLOCK buzzes at 7:00, waking me up from my deep, peaceful sleep. Still half asleep, I eat some toast and jam. After about thirty minutes of loitering in my bedroom, avoiding the fact that the Evaluation starts today, I decide to face my problem head-on. I drive to school slowly, quizzing myself on anything I can remember from prior years of experience and education. When I reach the building, I park my car and spot Clara standing in line near the gym doors.

"Clara, why are you in line?"

"We are getting our schedule for the week. You know, which group we are in and where we go each period."

We reach the front of the line quickly. There, sitting at a desk, is Luke.

"Name, please," he says without looking up.

"Clara Larson," Clara says.

"Here you go. You are in the first group of test takers today." He hands her a piece of paper with a schedule on it. After she grabs the paper, Clara walks a few feet away and waits for me.

"Name?"

"Kiara Smith."

"Okay. Here you go. This is your schedule for the next two days." When he hands me the piece of paper, Luke looks up at me. Our eyes lock, and he doesn't move. Our fingertips touch. He smiles for the briefest of moments and looks down, letting go of the paper. Everything is normal again, like nothing happened. I stumble over to Clara, who seems not to have noticed our little interaction.

"What group are you in?" she asks.

"Group two in the cafe. What about you?"

"Group one in the cafe. I really wish we were in the same group."

Ms. Cassini, who is holding the microphone, interrupts me by saying, "Group one, head on over to your designated rooms. Group two, please make your way out to the football field, where you will wait for group one to finish. Good luck!"

Before she leaves for the cafe, I look over at Clara one last time. "Good luck!"

After that, I make my way to the football field. It is humid outside, and sweat drips down the back of my neck. There are tents set out for us, so I sit under the tent closest to the end zone.

The short girl who asked the questions from the back of the crowd sits down next to me. Her name is Emerson.

"Are you ready for the test?" she says.

"Yes," I reply. Even though I am too nervous to talk, it is better to keep my mind off of the test.

"I am so excited about the test. Last night, I studied so much and even looked over my notebooks from freshman year. Did you study at all?" she asks.

"No. When I got home, I went straight to sleep because I was so tired. How did you stay awake?" I ask.

"Encouragement, perseverance, and a little bit of coffee."

We both laugh and continue talking. After about an hour and forty-five minutes, Luke walks out onto the field, holding a megaphone. "Group two, you will be taking your test early. The other groups finished a couple of minutes ago, so you will be able to start earlier. Girls head to the cafe. Boys head to the gym." Once he is finished talking, Luke walks back to the gym. He must be proctoring the boys' test.

The crowd of girls, including me and Emerson, quickly walk to the cafe. There, Lora is standing at the front of the room. "Take a seat, girls." After everyone finds a seat, she begins talking again. "You will have two hours to complete this assessment. It will test your prior knowledge along with material you have not covered in school. Try your best, and good luck."

Immediately, ten men, dressed in all white, walk through the aisles and place tests on each girl's desk. A man places the test on my desk.

At first glance, the test doesn't seem too hard. As I look through the first few pages, I see glimpses of trigonometry, history, and physics. Lots of stuff I know. When I flip to the last few pages, my jaw drops. It has questions about networking and about personal health and hygiene. We were never taught how to cure a cold. Why would they ask us this? These are questions for a doctor.

Oh, I get it. If you know these, then you might be well-suited for the job of a doctor. *Okay. Focus.* One by one, I answer all the questions. Mass-energy Equivalence is $E = mc^2$. A broken arm should be set before it is wrapped in gauze. The cerebrum is the part of the brain that controls thinking. The second President of the United States of America was John Adams.

Eventually, I reach the last question: If you could be in any profession, what would it be? Now that I think about it, I don't know. I could be an engineer, a doctor, or a professional sports player. Or perhaps a builder, a teacher, or a businesswoman. There are so many options. How could I choose one? After all, the test is supposed to reveal what profession I am best suited for. I'll just answer with, "I don't know."

Perfect. Done. Once I double-check my answers, I rise and walk to the front of the room. As I reach the front, I glance around the room. About half of us are finished. I place the test in front of Lora and walk back to my desk. A sense of relief washes over me. That wasn't so bad. It certainly could have been worse. How did Clara do?

When everyone finishes, we are allowed to leave. Lora told us Ms. Cassini was busy and couldn't give us a 'Good job' speech. I'm glad she's busy because I could not sit through another speech right now.

The drive home is quick and uneventful. While driving, I ponder the questions that were offered and the answers I put on the test. It is strange that they asked us which job we would like to have. I always assumed that your test and training results determined what job you received, and there was really no personal choice involved in the decision.

Hoping to chat with Clara for an hour or two, I stop by her house on the way home. By the time I get to my house, it's already 6:00 p.m. When I walk through the door, Mom has spaghetti on the table. The aroma fills the room.

"Perfect timing, Kiara. I was about to dish out the spaghetti on our plates," Mom says as I walk into our house. Jacob, my parents, and I sit down at the table and begin eating. My stomach grumbles, revealing how hungry I am. "I thought you would be hungry. Is it good?" she asks.

"Mmm. Delicious," I say through a mouthful of food.

"How is Clara?" Before I left school, I texted Mom that I was going to drop by her house. She loves Clara like a daughter, and Mrs. Larson feels the same way about me.

"She's good. We just sat in her room, chatted, and rested for a few hours. We were both wiped out from the last two days." I take another big bite of food. "Dad? Do you like being in a business job? Do you regret making that choice?"

"No, I don't regret it. It is fun, and it provides a good life for my family. Why do you ask?" he replies.

"Starting these tests has me wondering which jobs I would like to try."

"Kiara, you should be a police officer. They get to carry guns and stuff," Jacob says as he shovels more food into his mouth. Ever since he was young, Jacob has wanted to be a police officer. For his fourteenth birthday, my dad gave him a pellet gun. It's no wonder that now, at 16, he still wants to be one.

"I'll think about it, Jacob." After taking a sip of water, I continue saying, "Y'all are friends with some Brawn people, right?" They nod their heads in unison. "Which jobs do you think are better? Which jobs would suit me best?"

"Honey, I know you're worried. In fact, we all were at this age. However, there is no need to stress or even grill your parents with questions." Dad winks at me. "Just trust the test. It will show you all of your strengths and weaknesses, and it will guide you to make the right choice." Although you wouldn't expect it, my dad is just as comforting as my mom.

"But what if I do poorly on both tests? What if the Evaluation doesn't work on me?" That is one of my greatest fears. Being the one person who doesn't fit anywhere. I will become homeless, have no job, and be shunned by both the Brawn and the Brain.

"That's not going to happen, Kiara. Stop stressing over it." My mom always tries to cheer me up. Plus, she is almost always right, so I try to push aside that fear for now. "Now, you need to get some sleep. You have a big day tomorrow."

After taking a few more bites of food, I rise from the table and wash my dishes. Sleep slowly drags my eyes down. As soon as my head hits the pillow, I'm dead asleep.

CHAPTER 3

A NEW DAY always comes with a new challenge. In this case, it's my physical test. My schedule says my first section is learning techniques from Grey Canner. Who is Grey Canner? Then, I have endurance training, followed by the fighting section. Finally, I get a break. It will be nice to have a break in my last section.

On my way out the door, I grab a protein bar. Turning up the radio, I drive to school and park my car in front of the gym.

Clara stands near the doors of the gym, waiting for me. "Are you ready for today? I think we are in the same group."

"I hope I'm ready. Are you in Group 3?"

"Yes!"

"Yay!" We both let the excitement hang around for a few more seconds before facing the gym.

As we start walking towards the gym, a voice over the PA system announces, "All groups, head to your first section immediately." Clara and I continue walking to the gym as the other girls in our group do likewise. Standing in front of the gym doors is an older man wearing gym shorts and a tank top. He has a small scar near the right side of his lip, forcing the crease of his lip down. His face is stern with his arms crossed, suggesting he is a grumpy old man.

"My name is Grey Canner. Seventeen years of my life have been spent as a personal security guard for the President of the United States. Today, I will teach you the basic techniques for punching, knife throwing, and more. You will listen to me, watch me do it, and then try the motions for yourself. Towards the end of this session, you will practice the moves on a dummy or a partner. Understand?"

He is answered with silence as we all blankly stare at him. "I said, 'Do you understand?" he repeats.

We all snap to attention and respond with, "Yes, sir!"

Once we are all clustered inside the gym, he yells, "You have five seconds to get in front of a dummy. One person per dummy. Five, four. Three, two. One." Everyone is behind a dummy, waiting for his next order. My dummy is next to Clara's, which I am grateful for. "Congratulations, everyone. You can move your feet."

Mr. Canner looks us over as if he is sizing us up. This must be what the military is like. "First, you will learn the basics of punching. Look at my posture, how I hold my arms, my stance, where my body is facing relative to my target. Watch me closely."

He mimics a punch, lightly touching the target with his clenched fist, and repeats this action multiple times.

Each time, I focus on something else: his stance, where his feet are, how he holds his arms. After we have studied each part of the punch, he tells us to punch the dummy with the correct technique. While we practice punching, Mr. Canner walks around and critiques the girls' movements. When he walks past me, he stops for a few seconds. Trying to ignore him, I continue with the motions as if he wasn't there. "What's your name, young lady?"

"Kiara Smith." Looking him directly in the eyes, I search for signs of approval or dislike. After a few seconds, I look away and continue punching the dummy, but he doesn't move on.

"What are your parents' jobs?" he asks.

"My dad is a businessman, and my mom was an engineer," I say. *Why would he ask me about that? That's strange.*

"Hmm. Well, your form and technique are perfect. Keep up the good work." He continues on to the next few girls without another word.

Clara gives me a confused look, so I shrug my shoulders at her and keep punching. That's weird. Despite any urge I have ever had in the past, I've never actually punched someone before. Further, being in a family from the Intelligence category means no one has ever complimented me for being physically outstanding. It felt nice.

Mr. Canner teaches us a few more maneuvers: how to kick someone, how to escape from a chokehold, how to throw a knife, and how to carry and shoot a gun. For some reason, these all come easily to me. Even though I am a fast learner, this feels too natural. It's like I already know how to do each motion.

When it comes time for partners, I am partnered up with a girl named Clarisse. She has deep brown hair and green eyes and is a couple of inches taller than me. In high school, Clarisse was on the track team. "How's your test going?" she asks me.

"It's different from what I expected, but I am doing good so far. What about you?"

"From what I can tell, it's going well, but who knows what the results will look like."

"All right, ladies, you will demonstrate punching, kicking, and escaping from a chokehold on your partner. Assuming none of you want to walk away from this section with bruises, don't actually hit them unless you want to be hit that hard yourself. Please just tap your partner. When you reach the chokeholds, the person performing the chokehold will place their arm around the neck like so." He demonstrates this by wrapping his arm around a dummy's neck and placing the inside of his elbow just under where the chin would be. "Do each move five times. Go!"

About one hour is left in the section; Mr. Canner likes to move fast. Before I can think of anything else, Clarisse starts the motions of the punch. I ready myself and feel the tap of her closed fist in the middle of my chest. My turn. Placing my feet shoulder-width apart, I put my hands up by my face. When I am balanced, I step forward and throw my right hand forward. Before my hand collides with her chest, I stop it and barely tap her.

We repeat this a few more times before moving on to kicks. Spreading my feet shoulder width apart again, I slowly put all of my weight on my left foot. Then, I force my right foot to Clarisse's side, stopping inches from her and barely tapping her. Clarisse repeats the move, leaning on her left foot and stopping her right foot inches from my side. One more move: chokeholds. Clarisse goes first, so I wrap my arm around her neck, careful to place the inside of my elbow under her chin just as Mr. Canner showed us. Clarisse pulls my arm down, twists it, and pins it behind my back.

Now, it's my turn. She wraps her arm around my neck as I take a deep breath. One, two. Three. As soon as I pull her arm down, I slide my head through the gap. Then I twist her arm, pinning it against her back. We continue doing this for a few minutes until Mr. Canner calls us over.

"There are about 40 minutes left in this section. To end it, you will first show your ability to throw three knives. Then, we will move on to shooting. You will carry a gun ten yards, shoot a target three times, and carry the gun back. Got it? Good. Line up in a single file line behind the table with knives on it."

Although I didn't notice before, on the right side of the gym is a table that holds three knives. In front of it, there is a round target with three concentric circles. As Mr. Canner commanded us, we line up behind the table. I am about tenth in line, with Clara right behind me.

Slowly, the line progresses. The first person misses the target once and hits it on the edges with her second two throws. More people miss and hit the target, but only a few hit the bullseye once or twice. No one hits the bullseye all three times. The person in front of me misses the target two out of the three times.

My turn. I pick up a knife in my right hand and place the other two in my left. Turning it over in my hand a couple of times, I notice that it is heavier than I thought it would be but light enough to throw. It balances perfectly in my hand. Just like Mr. Canner showed us earlier, I carefully position the knife in my hand and throw it at the target. The tip of the blade hits the bullseye.

The look on my face reveals my shock. Clara, who is standing right behind me, looks just as shocked as I feel. When I throw the second knife, it is faster and with more confidence—a bullseye. Taking a deep breath, I pick up my final knife and prepare to throw it. After I release the knife, I watch it hurdle towards the target—another bullseye. The throw felt so instinctive that, momentarily, I believed I had experienced it before. *Impossible.* The only knives I have even touched are intended for cutting food.

All eyes follow me as I collect my knives. Only one person has gotten two bullseyes, and I know she has been throwing knives for fun since she was ten. No one else has thrown three bullseyes.

After Clara finishes, she rushes over to me. "Who knew you could throw a knife like that? You're a natural!"

"Thanks, but it's a shock to me, too." The thrill of throwing three bullseyes still grips me. I want to keep throwing, to keep proving that I am stronger than they believe. "But Clara, you got two on the target. Plus, one of them was centimeters away from the bullseye. That's really good!"

"Yeah, yeah. Not as good as three, though." A hint of jealousy grips her voice, but a smile spreads across her face. Nothing will ever get in between our friendship.

Once everyone is finished with knife throwing, we move on to shooting. Mr. Canner places a gun on top of the table and moves the target back another twenty-five yards. It is now forty yards in front of the table. When we line up, I end up in the front because no one else wanted to go first. Mr. Canner briefly reminds us how to hold and shoot a gun and informs us that this is an AR-15. He then waves his hand forward, indicating that I can start.

After picking up the gun, I adjust it to rest on my shoulder. It is heavy, but I can still carry it without much struggle. Then, I walk forward fifteen yards in front of the table and kneel, placing my elbow on my knee. When the crosshairs in the scope are aligned with the target, I breathe in, squeeze the trigger, and breathe out.

After I shoot three bullets, I stand up and walk back to the table, carefully placing the gun on it. When I look at the target, I see three holes in the bullseye. My jaw drops. *How did I just do that?*

Clara's eyes are round with shock. We both know that I have never touched a gun in my life, let alone shot one. The pistol my dad gave Jacob is the closest I have ever been to a real gun.

After a quick complimentary nod, Mr. Canner replaces the target and watches the next person pick up the gun. When Clara finishes shooting, she runs over to me. "How did you do that? It's like your inner abilities are coming out."

"I don't know. It is crazy how accurate I am with weapons I have never touched." The rest of the section goes by quickly as Clara and I talk. Most of the girls hit the target twice, and some get a bullseye. Once more, I am the only person to hit three bullseyes.

Then, we are called over to the football field for our endurance section. There, Lora waits with her arms crossed. The look of annoyance on her face suggests how the boys in the previous section were acting.

"Welcome to the endurance section. Let's get right into it. You will run two laps around the track and then complete thirty push-ups and thirty sit-ups." The command is met with blank stares. "Now!"

We immediately start running. Even though I have not been the best endurance runner in the past, I am one of the first to finish the laps. My heart is racing, but I am not tired. I feel alive. The push-ups and sit-ups are easy. My muscles burn, but I can easily push through it. Doing P.E. in high school prepared me for this short workout. When I finish, I stand up and shake out my tired arms.

As I look around, I see that I am the only one finished. Lora stands off to the side, watching us, most likely grading us on when we finish. Taking a seat in the shade, I wait for the rest of the girls to finish the exercise. Clara finishes around twentieth place. "How was it, Clara?"

"As good as it could be." In an attempt to catch her breath, she leans over and puts her hands on her knees. "I mean, I never liked P.E., so this is not my favorite thing in the world."

Before I can respond, Lora starts speaking. "Well done, everyone. You can get five minutes to rest, but no more. The relay race is next up." We all sit down and chat for five minutes, resting our bodies and calming our breaths. Before standing up again, I chug a small water bottle.

"Five minutes is up. You have been divided up into five teams for the relay race. Come see them and figure out your order. Each person will run twice. Half of you are on one side of the field, and the other half of you are on the other side of the field. Go!" Most of the people that I recognize on my team are sports players who will ultimately help us win the race.

If this were a typical relay race, one where just a bunch of friends were playing around, I would be relaxed. However, because this is part of our evaluation, I set my jaw—determined to win! As my competitive nature takes over, I gear up for the race.

After debating the running order, I end up second in line. Lora blows the whistle, and our first runner starts sprinting towards me. Ten feet away. Five feet. One foot.

My legs start sprinting as I grab the baton. Since I am the third one to receive the baton, I have to make up some time. As I run, I hear my heartbeat in my ears. I take shallow breaths as I push myself. I pass one girl. One more to go. I run as fast as I have ever run before. When I reach the other side of the field, I hand the baton off to my partner at the same time as my opponent does. We are both tied for first place.

My heart pounds in my chest. My adrenaline is high, and my face feels windblown. Only five minutes remain until I have to run again. Sitting on the grass, I focus on my breathing. Our team hands off the baton and sprints to the other side of the field. We maintain our lead for many laps, but then an opposing team catches up to us.

It is my turn to run again. When the baton is in my hands, I sprint at full speed. My team is in second place by a few feet, so I use all of my strength to run as fast as I can. I hand off the baton just a few seconds before the other team. The race continues, and in the end, my team wins by a couple of inches. We did it. We won the race!

"Good job, ladies. You all did well. Take a couple of minutes to catch your breath before the next section. Hopefully, I will see you soon."

CHAPTER 4

DUE TO OUR high school's wrestling team being second in the state, we have a dedicated practice building for them. It has two wrestling rings for fighting and punching bags lining the walls. However, I never knew it was used for testing.

When we walk into the building, I find Luke standing in the middle of the first ring. Butterflies fill my stomach. Why am I nervous? As soon as I look at Luke, the feeling gets worse. It's Luke. Luke makes me feel giddy inside. I can't deal with this right now; I have to focus on the test.

"Hello. As you all know, you will be fighting today. Since I can't fight fifty of you in two hours, we will be splitting you up. My friend Zachary has offered to help out." As he says this, a man around the same age as Luke walks into the ring. "Zach will only push you as hard as I say. This will allow us to fight each of you for four and a half minutes and give you critiques. If you are not fighting, I advise you to practice on the punching bags. We will split you up by first name. A through M, you are with me. N through Z, please follow Zach to the next ring. Okay? Good. Angelina, you're up first."

The fights drag by slowly. Since my name starts with "K," I will be the third to last one to fight Luke. After practicing some kicks and punches on the punching bag, I decide to wait it out. Clara fights Luke well, but still ends up pinned on the ground. Time passes by, then I hear Luke yell, "Kiara Smith!"

Giving myself a mini pep talk, I walk into the ring and get into a fighting stance. Luke makes the first move, punching at my head. At the last second, I duck. "Nice sidestep," he says. Instead of responding, I pull my leg up to kick him and nail him in the side.

"Sorry, I didn't mean to hurt you."

"Never say sorry. Keep fighting." Despite Luke's quick moves, I block his kick with my hand and pull him from his feet. "So, you know how to fight. That means I can go harder on you." Before I can tell him that I have never fought anyone before, he lunges at me like a leopard. Luke's body hits mine, and we fall to the floor. Once he positions himself behind my back, he wraps his elbow around my neck.

My heart is racing, and I start to panic. The pounding in my ears grows louder. Fear grips me, as I do not want to suffocate. Then, I remember what we practiced earlier in the techniques section. Pulling his arm slightly forward, I slip my head through the gap.

After I am free, I yank Luke's arm around his back and pin him on the ground.

"I win."

"Really?" Luke replies sarcastically. As soon as I loosen my grip, he whirls around and pins me to the floor. "I win."

Desperation rises in me as I attempt to free myself. I could give up, or I could try to kick him. Giving up is never an option, so I have to kick him. Taking a few deep breaths, I pull my knee up and hit something soft, probably his stomach. Luke flinches, and his body buckles. When he stands up, he moves his hands to the place where I kicked him.

In a strained voice, he says, "Most girls give up when they are pinned." He stares at me for a few seconds, then snaps out of his daze.

Feeling a little awkward, I walk toward him. "Did I hurt you? I'm so sorry. To be honest with you, I didn't even know I could do that." I touch his back and then freeze. Am I flirting with my instructor? Luke doesn't move either but doesn't pull away from my hand. Keeping my hand on his back, I start rubbing it. That's a casual move, right? Our eyes meet, and we stare at each other for a second that feels like an eternity.

Luke glances at my hand, which is rubbing his back. My face gets hot; I hope he doesn't notice. My eyes fall to the floor as my hand drops to my side. "I'm sorry," I repeat. "Do you need ice? Can I get you anything?"

"No. I'm fine, thanks," he wheezes. Guilt rises in me. It never occurred to me that I could ever cause pain like this, physical pain.

After a few moments of awkward silence, I walk him over to the benches where he sits down. Should I leave or sit down next to him? When I start to move away, he stops me. "Wait with me, will you?"

My cheeks feel hot, and I start to blush again. Act cool, Kiara. This is my instructor. Honestly, he probably just thinks of me as another silly girl. "Okay. Are you feeling any better?"

"Not really, but I need to go test two more girls. Stay here after the section, okay?" His face is serious but not stern. Searching for more words, he decides to drop his eyes to the floor and wait for my answer.

"Sure." I smile as he walks back into the ring. Besides bending over slightly, you would never be able to tell he just got kicked in the gut. The next two fights fly by. My eyes follow Luke as I watch his every move in the ring.

When everyone finishes fighting, we all gather in the ring around Luke and Zach. "Good job, ladies. You all did well. Your next section is a break, so you may go anywhere on campus except for the gym, the football field, and this building. That's all for today. Have a good afternoon." All the girls leave. Clara looks back at me, but I wave her on. I will catch up with her later.

When Zach walks back to the locker room, I approach Luke. "How's your side?"

"It'll be fine." A grin spreads across his face, and he looks me straight in the eyes. "Where'd you learn to fight like that?"

"All of this came naturally to me. It's really weird. It was like that during techniques, too. My shooting felt natural even though I have never shot a gun before. Isn't that weird?

"Yeah." Luke seems spaced out like he's thinking about something monumental.

"I'm sorry. Did I say something wrong? Trust me, I'm not normally this open. Usually, I only share things with people I trust or like, or...." I realize what I just said. I just admitted to liking him. Color fills my cheeks, and my palms get sweaty.

His eyes drop to the ground, and my eyes follow them. Luke heard it. He chuckles to himself before continuing. "You're fine. I was just wondering if you were—never mind. Are you feeling okay? When I put you in a chokehold, I think I squeezed you too hard."

"I'm good." As I look down, I notice his hand is still holding his side. "Are you sure you're okay? I feel so bad about kicking you."

Luke places his hand under my chin and lifts my head so we are staring at each other. My stomach is twirling, and nervous energy is running through my body. I try not to focus on the place where his hand touches me. "Look. You're fine. Stop apologizing. You did what you were told to do."

His hand drops back to his side, but the nervous energy remains in my body. It's just a casual gesture, but it means so much more to me. "Now, I have to go test the next group. The five minutes between sections is almost up. I'll see you later, okay?"

"Okay." My heart flutters.

Once he turns around, I leave the building just as a crowd of boys walks into the gym. Once outside, I half walk and half skip to the cafe where most of the girls are talking. Clara is sitting on a bench, talking to Clarisse and a girl named Susan from my social studies class. When our eyes meet, she says something to the two girls and walks up to me. We find a table near the wall.

"Why did you stay back?"

"Luke just wanted to ask me something. Were you talking to Susan?"

"Yeah. She's always so nice, but don't change the subject. What did Luke ask you?"

"He just wanted to know where I was trained to fight. Of course, I said I wasn't trained anywhere." Before Clara can say anything else, I change the subject. Right now, I don't want to talk about Luke. I don't know how I feel about him yet. *Do I like him? Does he think of me as a little girl?* "How did your fight go?"

"Good. Luke pinned me pretty quickly, but I got a few good hits. I noticed you won."

"Yeah, but it was really all luck." At this, we both smile. We continue talking for the rest of our break, but I can't stop thinking about my fight. How did I beat him? My moves just came so naturally. How is that possible?

Ms. Cassini gives a speech at the end of the day. My mind is busy with Luke and other things, so I don't listen. My head is filled with so many mixed feelings that I become tired and dizzy. After the speech, I drive home quickly and go straight to bed.

CHΛPTER 5

AFTER A RESTLESS night, I wake up to sweaty palms. Today is personality testing day. These results can't be bad, right? It's just testing our personality. I'll be fine. Trying to take my mind off of this test, I head downstairs and grab a banana. After eating it and grabbing my bag, I catch my mom on the way out of the door.

"Mom, is the personality test easy? Do you think I'll be fine?"

"Honey, you'll do great. Do not worry about it. I love you." Mom kisses my forehead and wraps me in a hug. However, her calm nature does not ease my racing heart today.

"Mom, I love you too."

When I arrive at school, I notice there is a crowd by the door. When I park my car, Clara meets me with an uneasy smile. "Are you ready?"

"As ready as I'll ever be. What about you?" she asks.

"I'm ready. Hopefully, today won't be as intense. They are just testing our personality, right? It shouldn't be that hard."

"I don't know, Kiara. Most of the people in Brawn and Brain training say this is the worst part or the easiest part. There's no in-between. You love it, or you hate it." Lines of worry spread across Clara's face.

"Clara, don't worry. That's coming from a bunch of kids with new jobs who just want to make some trouble. We'll be fine." Her face lightens up a bit. As we walk to the gym, I try to take my own advice and not worry.

Two lines have started forming in front of the gym doors: girls on the right and boys on the left. Clara and I hop into our respective lines. Today, they are handing out information about the personality test. For security reasons, no information can be released prior to the test day. So, we have no idea what to expect and no idea when we are taking it. The line progresses slowly until Clara is the only one in front of me. Following suit, Clara accepts her paper.

Once she moves out of the way, I walk up to Lora, who is sitting behind a table with a stack of papers in front of her. Luke is sitting on her right with a different stack of papers. Without looking up, Lora asks, "Name, please?"

"Kiara Smith." Luke grins but does not look up. What does that mean? Lora draws my attention back to her when she hands me a piece of paper. "Thank you."

As I walk towards Clara, I hear a faint, "You're welcome."

"What time is your test?" asks Clara.

"I don't know; I haven't even looked." As soon as I look down at my paper, I see a list of words near the top. Name, age, gender. Then, I see 'TIME' written in all capital letters. "Mine's at 10:30. What about you?"

"11:30. Lora is administering mine. She's nice. Who's doing yours?"

Skimming farther down the page, I see "Administrator" next to the word "Luke Johnson." Luke is administering my test. The Luke that I beat in fighting yesterday. The Luke that makes my heart flutter and my pulse quicken. That Luke. "Luke is administering mine."

"That's scary."

"Why?"

"Luke acts so tough. It's a little intimidating, don't you think?"

Right now, I don't want to argue with her, so I simply agree. "Yeah, I guess so."

Suddenly, a voice rings throughout the room, saying, "Hello, ladies and gentlemen!" Ms. Cassini stands at the front of the room, holding a microphone. "Today is the last day of testing. You will go into your allotted classroom and meet your instructor. Lora, Luke, and Mr. Canner are joining us today, along with some of your former teachers. Each test will take about thirty minutes. This will go on from 9:00 AM to 2:00 P.M.. If it's not your turn, you will remain in the gym. After the test, you will head to the cafeteria to wait for everyone to finish. Lunch will be provided for those who have finished. Thank you!"

Ms. Cassini walks out the door, followed by all the instructors. There are a total of twenty instructors, meaning each one will have to administer ten tests. That would be an exceptionally long day. Test after test from 9:00 in the morning to 2:00 in the afternoon. Endless testing.

"So, what should we do while we wait?" Clara asks.

"Let's look over our sheet." I skip the general information about me, like my name and age, and read about my test. It will take place in the junior history classroom from 10:30 to 11:00, and Luke Johnson will administer it.

Time passes. There's not much to say when your character is about to be judged and scored on a test you will take in less than one hour. Clara and I sit in silence and think. Forty-five minutes left. Thirty minutes. Ten minutes.

"If you are taking the test at 10:30, head to your designated classroom," someone says over the PA system.

"Good luck, Kiara."

"Thanks, Clara. Good luck to you, too." Getting up from my seat, I walk out of the gym with twenty other people, butterflies forming in my stomach. After we leave the gym, we all go our separate ways. In my case, I head to the history classroom. My heart is racing, my breath quickens, and anxiety starts to kick in. *Calm down, Kiara. It's just a test.* I just have to get through it with a calm attitude. When I reach the history classroom, I try to slow my breathing.

After a few seconds, I knock on the door. "Come in," Luke says. Following his instruction, I enter the classroom. Luke is cleaning something that looks like a pair of oversized goggles. When he looks up at me, he smiles, and I can't help but grin, too. "Have a seat, please."

I walk over to the chair and sit down. It looks like a dentist's chair, and I remember when I got my braces off in seventh grade. Back then, I was so excited. Now, my stomach is practically in my throat, and my hands won't stop shaking. "Luke, were you nervous when you took this test?"

"Not really." His eyes meet mine, and a smile spreads across his face. He looks like he is trying to reassure me, but it is not working. My heart is beating fast. "Don't worry. You'll do fine." Luke finishes cleaning the goggles and then hands them to me. "Put these on. The whole virtual reality test will take place in your head, and the image will be portrayed in these goggles. I can't tell you anything else."

"How long will it take?" I ask.

"Sorry, but I can't tell you right now. Please, just put the headset on." Before I slip the goggles on, I see him dabbing a cloth with some kind of liquid. Once the goggles are on, a cloth suddenly covers my nose and mouth. I panic. "Calm down, Kiara. It's just me," Luke says.

Leaning back in the chair, I try to relax. Luke clicks a button, and everything goes black. My body slowly relaxes, and I notice whatever is on that cloth is pulling me to sleep or something else. I close my eyes. *Relax, Kiara.*

When I open my eyes, I find a boy staring back at me. I'm no longer in the classroom but in the courtyard in front of our school. That boy is so familiar; he was the sophomore bully. I hated him then, and I hate him now. This kid left such a negative impact on our school, even after he transferred to our rival school.

To my right, a small boy crouches on the ground. His sweaty brown hair sticks to the side of his head, and he is holding his face in his hands. When he shifts, I see a mixture of blood and tears soaking his face and his hands. The bully's knuckles are split. I connect the dots, realizing he punched the kid in the nose. The bully starts toward the boy with closed fists again. I can't watch this; I won't let it happen.

As soon as he is within a few feet of me, I lunge at the bully, but arms come out from nowhere and constrict me. Even though they are invisible, they are strong enough to hold me back. The bully, realizing my inability to move, turns to me. "You think you're so tough for standing up for this kid? Hate to break it to you, but you're not. You're the weakest kid in the grade. My seven-year-old sister could beat you in a fight. You are *worthless*."

I close my eyes. Calm yourself, Kiara. He is just trying to aggravate you. Ignore him. Concentrate. Ignore him.

He takes a few more steps in my direction. "You have *no* friends. You are *not* popular. *No one* likes you. You are a needy, dejected little girl and a disgrace to your family."

As the words fill my head, I throw my body towards him. The arms around me tighten, further constricting me.

"I could never live like you."

Suddenly, I stop. This kid is just an insecure boy trying to get inside of my head. Why am I letting him in? Determined to calm down, I take a few breaths and turn away. Then I walk away as he taunts and mocks me. When I reach the little boy crouching on the ground, I gently touch him on the shoulder.

"Are you okay?" I whisper into his ear.

The boy nods his head. I help him to his feet and start walking back towards the school. Hopefully, the nurse will be able to take care of him.

"Coward! You shy away from danger! You are *worthless*." The bully's hands are in the air as he spits these words at me.

Despite trying to ignore him, I flinch in his direction, eager to punch his front teeth out. However, I have to remain calm and focus on my mission of getting this boy to the nurse.

The arms that restrained me finally disappear as we open the doors to the school, and the building I have seen every single day for the last four years quickly changes to a prison. The boy disappears as I shift my attention elsewhere. Behind the bars of a prison cell, Clara sits on a bench alone. Confused, I move toward her, but I am stopped by a man in a black suit. "Do you know this criminal? She was found guilty of murder and is sentenced to a lifetime in prison."

I'm stunned. Clara, the happy and joyful girl I know, killed someone? How can I be friends with a murderer? But it's Clara, my best friend. What should I say? Tears well up in my eyes. I look at her, asking if this is true. Clara nods her head.

"Answer me! Do you know her?"

"Umm, I do ..." Clara stares at me and shakes her head. She doesn't want me to get in trouble because I know her. Despite being in jail, she is trying to save me.

"How?" He yells at me. "This girl is wanted in five different countries for murder. We are looking for an accomplice, and you're becoming a pretty good option."

"I—I do not. You didn't let me finish. I don't know her; I'm sorry." The lie lingers in the air. Clara saved me, but should I have told the truth? Should I have stayed true to my friend or obeyed the law? Clara looks at me, sadness filling her eyes. She mouths the words, "I'll be fine," but I can't ignore the pang of guilt for leaving her here. One way or another, I'll get her out of prison.

When I leave the prison, I see an old man in ragged clothes rummaging through a garbage can, looking for some food. An apple instantly appears in my pocket. Should I give it to him or look away and keep walking? He looks up and stares at me for a few seconds. His eyes bore into my soul, and I feel like he is reading my mind. "Do you have any food?" His voice is harsh as if he has been screaming for over two hours.

Should I give it to him? My parents always said to help the poor in any way you can, but countless images of violence rack my mind. Why am I even questioning this? It should be such an easy decision. I toss him the apple, and he gives me a grateful smile. Gaps show in between his crooked teeth. One of his front teeth is missing.

"Thank you." Turning away from me, he takes a big bite of the apple.

As I walk away, a feeling of relief washes over me because I did something good. After a few more yards, I find myself in a race. I am one hundred yards away from the finish line, and someone just passed me. Why are they running? Signs all around me say, "If you win, you will save your family from death."

How did I get in this race? When I look towards the finish line, I see Mom, Dad, and Jacob lined up at gunpoint. This race is serious; I won't let my family die. So, I run. Each step burns me and drags me down. Each step sets my heart on fire. Each step pains me to the point that tears well up in my eyes, and I start screaming. But each step reminds me that I must run for my family. It feels like fire sears my skin, and my arms turn a bright pink color.

My eyes are now watering. My family still stands at the finish line, holding hands. They are staring at me, smiling. Jacob is cheering me on. I won't let them die. I endure the pain, using it as fuel. My opponent is a couple of steps in front of me. A couple more steps. More pain. The finish line is so close. Two more steps. Two more moments of pain. I pass my opponent and make it to the finish line. My family is safe.

Finished with the race, I run up to hug my family, but they fade away. Where did they go?

The pain fades as I walk into a classroom full of students. Each student is staring me down with hungry eyes. To my left, a professor stands behind a podium. Where am I? "Ms. Smith, this is your final question. If you answer correctly, you are free to leave. If you answer incorrectly, you will have to spend an eternity rotting in this classroom, never allowed to leave."

That's intense. Surely, he can't be serious. By the way, the students are staring at me, and I can tell he is dead serious. "Your question is, 'How old are the oldest fossils on Earth?' You have one minute, starting now."

Feeling the pressure, I rack my brain. This is such a random question, but I must know something about fossils. We learned about fossils in seventh grade. There are many dinosaur fossils on Earth. Dinosaurs are really old, but there are more than dinosaur fossils. There are bacteria fossils.

"Thirty seconds."

My heart is racing. I can't be stuck here. What about my family? Moments ago, I ran through searing pain for them. What about my friends? I can do this; I have to do this. *Think, Kiara, think.* At least three billion years old.

"Ten. Nine."

3.1 billion? No. 3.2 billion?

"Five. Four."

3.5 billion years?

"Three. Two."

Yes. "3.5 billion years old."

"That is correct! Good job. You are free to leave."

Everything goes black. I open my eyes and yank the goggles off. After I adjust to the light, I push myself out of the chair and walk a few paces away. Putting my hands over my face, I walk back toward the chair. My breaths are shallow, and my heart is pounding in my chest. Luke is standing next to the chair, holding a glass of water. "Here. Drink this."

Grateful, I grab the water and start sipping it. "Thanks. I don't have to do that again, do I?"

Luke chuckles and looks up at me. "No. This is the only time."

"And is Clara actually in jail? How is that little boy?"

"None of that was real. They were all just scenarios created to test your reaction."

A sigh of relief escapes my mouth. I don't know what I would do without Clara. "So, how did I do?"

"Good." He pauses for a second. "Your test results were really interesting. They weren't bad, though. Quick question. Have you ever heard of the Amari?"

"No. Why?"

"Oh, no reason. Just a thought. Back to your earlier question: the amount of time each student takes to complete the tasks determines the total time of the test. Yours took ten minutes, about half the time of the average. You were incredibly fast. Is that a good enough answer?"

"Yes, but don't change the subject. What are the Amari?"

His attempt at a smile fades, and his face turns serious. "Tomorrow, you will get your results back. Ms. Cassini will most likely try to single you out. Whatever you do, stay with someone. Don't get singled out by her. Before you leave, come find me. Job selection is on Sunday, and I need to talk to you before then. Okay?"

"So, don't get singled out by Ms. Cassini, and make sure to find you before I leave. Got it. See you later." Without looking up at him, I start toward the door.

"One more thing." Luke looks me dead in the eyes and smiles. "Don't worry. You did great." Then, he proceeds to clean the goggles. I take that as my sign to leave.

When I leave the building, I find a few more students walking towards the cafe. They must have had the test at the same time I had mine. Wanting to process what just happened, I walk in silence to the cafe to wait.

When 12:00 p.m. arrives, Clara staggers over to me. She looks like she just made the most crucial decision of her life and failed. "Are you okay?"

"My test was brutal. I ignored so many homeless people. You know about my bad experiences with them, so there was no way I could even look them in the eyes." When Clara was little, she and her mom went for a walk out in the city. A homeless man started chasing them with a knife before someone else was able to stop him. Now, she avoids them at all costs.

"On top of that guilt, I had to watch a twenty-year-old bully beat up a child for no reason. It was awful. And then, I ignored you!

You were going to die, and they asked me if I knew you, and I..." she bursts into sobs. Placing my arm around her, I try to comfort her. My scenarios were remarkably similar to hers. The results must be based on the decisions we made. "And now, you probably think I am the worst friend ever." Tears stream down her face.

"Clara, listen to me. It is just a stupid test. After today, we won't ever have to think about it again." Her breaths slow down. "It doesn't mean anything."

"Will you forgive me?" Her eyes are red, but she has stopped crying.

"Of course. Plus, these situations make people do weird things."

"Thanks, Kiara." Clara leans into me, and we sit there next to each other, for several minutes. Once she calms down, we talk for the rest of the afternoon.

At 2:00 p.m., everyone finishes their test. Ms. Cassini calls us back into the gym, where she is holding a microphone. As soon as we are all settled, she begins talking. "Congratulations! You finished all of your tests. The next step will be meeting up with an instructor to get your results. Lora, Luke, Mr. Canner, and the other instructors will be sharing your results with you privately. Tomorrow will be the last day of testing and finishing your Evaluation. You will have Saturday off, and then the Selection will take place on Sunday. Get a good night's rest, and we will see you in the morning."

As she walks off the stage, I close my eyes and hear the tap of each heel hitting the floor. In two days, I can join my family and become a woman in Intelligence. Or I can leave them behind and pursue a more physical job.

Clara and I walk to our cars together and then drive home. The whole time, I think about what job I will get. It's 5:00 p.m. when my dad gets home from work. I set the table for dinner, and we all pile food onto our plates. "Dad, Mom, can I ask you a question about the personality test?"

"Sure. What do you need to know?" Dad takes a big bite of salad and looks up.

"The personality test evaluates how you react in different situations, right?"

"Right." He drags the word out, not looking up from his salad.

"So, technically, there is a 'good' way and a 'bad' way to react?"

"Technically. It is a scenario designed to see which option you will choose. For example, who you will stay loyal to or whether you pick your own safety over another's."

"Is it possible for someone to react to each scenario in a positive way? Everyone is flawed, so that means there must be at least *one* scenario we ignore or fail. During the test, I felt like I did everything right. I also didn't feel guilty when leaving the test. The only thing that left me uneasy was having to lie about my friendship with Clara, but that sounds like a scenario with two options showing where your loyalties lay."

Dad's hand, which was holding a spoon filled with soup, stops halfway in the air. His eyes widen, and his mouth absently closes and opens. His eyes look like they are searching for an answer.

Mom helps him out, saying, "Yes, I guess there is a chance that someone could react to all the scenarios positively."

My mom glances at my father and then looks back at me. Jacob and I are both confused. "Honey, I think you should rest tonight. Go to your room and get ready for bed. You have a big day tomorrow." She rises from her seat and gathers all of our dirty plates.

Not wanting to upset my mom, I get up and tell everyone, "Goodnight."

Still confused about why my parents acted so secretly, I go to bed. I drift into a deep sleep the moment my head touches my pillow.

CH∧PTER 6

WHEN I WAKE up, a feeling of uneasiness plagues my mind. They will give me my results today. What will they say? Which jobs will suit me best? Intelligence jobs? Vigor jobs?

After I walk downstairs and grab a protein bar, I wave to Mom and Jacob and start my drive to school. I need to busy my mind with something other than my results. Let's think about my family. This summer, I will leave them for training. Will I get to visit them? Will I get to see my friends? This isn't helping. My palms are already sweaty, and I feel my heart pounding in my chest. I haven't even arrived at school yet.

When I walk up to the gym building, a teacher stands at the door. "Find your seat. It has your name on it, along with what room your results will be shared."

As soon as I walk in, I find all the seats in the stands covered with slips of paper. In each row, there are twenty seats. There are ten rows, making the gym look like a sea of chairs. Turning into the "S" row, I find a slip of paper that says "Smith - Room 102." My seat is second from the left, and my row is third from the back. Clara is six rows in front of me.

Once we are all seated in our assigned spots, Ms. Cassini walks out carrying a microphone. "Today is the day you'll receive your results. We will call you in alphabetical order according to last name. Then, you will get twenty minutes with your instructor so that they can explain your results to you. Every row that is not being called can go do something else on campus. You must be back when your row is called. Samatha Adams, your row is first. Please go to your designated classrooms."

Since my last name is towards the end of the alphabet, I have time to roam around campus. I wish I had an "A" last name so that I could get this over with. Instead, I must wait for over two hours. Once I find Clara, we roam the campus together, waiting to be called.

"What do you think your results say?" she asks me.

"I don't know, but I think I did well in the physical tests. So, I might be more of a Brawn than a Brain."

"Same with me. As soon as the mental test was over, I knew I had bombed it. I didn't know half of the questions." Clara laughs lightly, but I can tell she is worried about her results.

"Hey, look at me. You're going to be fine." All she gives me is a pointed look before fading into a deep train of thought.

Despite my persistent nerves, I am not too worried. No matter where we end up, we will still be best friends, and I will still have my family. I can't help but wonder what my results are, though. What if I failed all the tests? What if I performed well on both tests?

About ten minutes before her row is called, Clara heads back to the gym. So, I am left alone with my thoughts. The stress begins to set in. Talking to Clara was comforting because it took my mind off of the upcoming results. Now, I start to overthink my tests. I decide to head back to the gym to wait the rest of the time. Hopefully, I can keep my mind off the tests.

My row is called. I stand up and get in line, following behind a boy named Daniel Sloan. We walk into a hallway and stand shoulder to shoulder. Then, the instructors walk out from a hallway to our right and approach their designated students. It just so happens that my instructor is Luke.

My heart flutters from both Luke and the anticipation of my test results waiting in Room 102. It is strange, though. Luke always ends up being my instructor. Is this a coincidence, or is he choosing me on purpose? I mean, I don't hate it. I'd rather it be him than a stranger.

Luke looks into my eyes and smiles. His deep blue eyes entrance me. They capture me in a world full of mystery. "Follow me." He leads me down the hallway and takes a left turn. When we reach Room 102, an old English classroom, he opens the door to let me in. As I walk in, he places his hand on the small of my back to guide me toward a desk. A shiver runs through me as he lifts his hand. Luke sits in a chair across from me, a table between us. He leans his elbows on the table and looks up at me.

"Your results were interesting. You should be glad I am the one delivering them to you and not one of Ms. Cassini's minions. Don't worry, you're safe here."

My stomach drops. That means something went wrong with my tests. Did I fail all three? Am I not cut out for any job? I try to put a smile on my face, but it doesn't work. "So, what's wrong with me?"

Luke looks confused; it's like I just said something to him in a foreign language. "Nothing's wrong with you."

I feel a little better. If nothing is wrong, what is he so worried about? "So, I guess I don't need to meet up with you later like you asked last night. I mean, you're giving me my results now, so you won't have to tell me anything later."

He ponders this for a second as if going over everything he would have told me. "Correct." His expression shifts to a more serious manner, and his smile fades. "Now, for your results. You got a 99% on your mental test. That is almost unheard of. Anything above a 90 is phenomenal. You just missed a question about some random virus and an animal species."

"Wait. Did you just say 99%? I didn't even know half of the questions on the test. How is that possible?"

Luke looks like he is about to say something, but then he changes his mind and starts with something else. "Well, your inner mind must have kicked in because you got everything right. Or you are really good at reasoning and eliminating illogical answers." Pausing for a brief second, he then moves on.

"Your physical test was perfect. Perfect techniques, perfect aim, perfect fighting skills. You also have high endurance." He looks me dead in the eyes. "And your personality is flawless. You did everything you were supposed to do. For example, you helped the poor, you stood up for the boy, everything. There was one instance, though, where you did not tell the truth.

"The point of that scenario was to see if you were honest, but you yielded to your friend's wish. In a way, you both failed *and* passed that scenario. Overall, your personality is very admirable. Do you know what this means?"

My heart pounds in my throat. I can hardly breathe. Dad said no one is flawless on their personality test. How is that possible?

"No."

"That means you are..." his voice drops to a whisper, "an Amari."

"What's an Amari?" That term feels strange on my lips. Familiar, but strange.

"Well, to begin, you must not tell anyone. Not your friends, not your family, no one. Some people think the Amari are dangerous because they are extremely good fighters and are incredibly smart. They can't be controlled because they have no weaknesses. There are little groups of them all over the country and the world. You can never actually tell them apart from others because they can blend in with regular people."

Luke pauses for a second, debating on whether to continue with this little history lesson. "You show all the signs of an Amari. Don't tell anyone under any circumstances. And never tell Ms. Cassini or anyone who works for her. Avoid her at all costs. Okay?"

My heart is pounding, and my head is spinning with all of this new information. "Okay. So, what should I pick for the Selection? Which area should I go into? Vigor or Intelligence?"

"That's your choice. An Amari excels in both areas but is generally higher in one or the other. You are outstanding in both, so it is your choice."

Something doesn't fit. How does he know so much about these so-called "Amari" unless he is one? "Wait—are you an Amari?"

A stunned expression replaces his innocent smile. He drops his eyes to the table and cracks his knuckles. "That's beside the point. I …"

"That means you are," I interrupt! "You evaded the question, which means you are concealing something. So, are you an Amari?"

Luke looks me dead in the eyes, and a stern expression engulfs his face. "If I was, I wouldn't tell you. If I wasn't, I would still not tell you. I am not opening up to some silly 18-year-old girl asking me questions. Understand?"

A weight drops in me. I thought he liked me; I thought we had something. In reality, I am just another girl hoping for something that won't ever happen. My eyes drop to the floor, and I fold my hands in my lap.

"Sorry." The hurt in his voice is evident. "I didn't mean to—I wasn't trying to be harsh."

I look up at him. His eyebrows are wrinkled, and his eyes are open wide.

"It's okay. Sorry for pushing you." His sudden outburst still shocks me.

"Please stay safe and remember to avoid Ms. Cassini."

As he waits for a response, I walk towards the door. Trying to put a smile on my face, I give him a curt "I will" and leave the room.

Once I'm in the hallway, it hits me. Amari. I will always be an Amari. This thing, this group, is now branded to me. I am different from my friends and from my family. Come to think of it, I will always be different. I will always be Kiara—an Amari!

Overwhelmed, I take a few seconds to process this news. That doesn't sound right. That can't be right. Luke was lying. This must be a test, right? How can I be an Amari if I have never even heard of them?

Being more confused than ever, I walk back into the gym and wait for the rest of the group to finish. Once everyone is done, Ms. Cassini walks out, holding a microphone. I must stay away from her even if I am not an Amari. The grave face that was on Luke's face confirms she is dangerous.

"Can everyone take their seats?" She takes a moment to let everyone calm down and locate their designated chairs. "Good job, students. The tests are over, and I am convinced that you all performed outstandingly. You may leave and never think about these tests again but think about your choices. Some of you might want to go into a physical-based job, while others of you prefer mental-based jobs. It's up to you. Think about it. In two days, the entire city will gather to watch your choices. Have a good night but be considerate about what you will choose."

As soon as Ms. Cassini finishes talking, the entire crowd floods out of the doors. Clara and I hang back for a moment, letting the group of kids slowly file out of the gym. Once the crowd has thinned out, we leave the building. I catch Luke looking at me and wave. His mouth twitches into a small grin, but he turns back to Lora and the rest of the instructors.

Luke wouldn't lie to me. Does that mean I really am an Amari?

CH/\PTER 7

SATURDAY FLIES BY. Throughout the day, I think about what I will choose and all the possible outcomes. Every now and then, Luke slips into my mind. Does he like me? Is he also an Amari? *Stay focused.* I have also accepted the fact that I am an Amari. Since I can't change that fact, I might as well embrace it.

However, my test results have left me in a gray area. If I excel in both the Mental and Physical sections, what should I choose? I could follow my parents and pursue a job in Intelligence or pave my own path in Vigor. There are so many options, so many possibilities. What will I choose? Plagued by my indecisiveness, I fall asleep early that night, wanting to get some rest before my big day.

My heart races when I wake up. Today is the Selection, and I still don't know what I will choose. Even though I'm nervous, I'm still excited about starting my life. Most people take off work to watch the Selection, noting where each teenager lands. The chairs are always full, and people end up standing at the edge of the big room to watch.

My dad drives us to City Hall, where the Selection takes place every year. We ride in silence, everyone absorbed in their own thoughts. I still haven't decided what I will choose. If I could just talk to Luke, then I could ask him more questions and get his opinion on my predicament.

When we arrive, my mom and dad give me a big hug. Jacob tells me, "Good luck," before they walk to find seats in the audience. City Hall is a giant building with white columns at its entrance. On the inside, there is a conference room that takes up most of the building. This is where the Selection is held. I stand among a group of twelfth graders who appear nervous, gathered by one of the side doors. Luke and the other instructors sort us by last name in alphabetical order. Despite my previous objection, I am now grateful to be toward the end, so I have more time to think about my choice.

When Luke is a couple of feet away, I try to catch his attention. "Luke!"

He looks at me and walks over. "What do you need? I am not allowed to talk to you right now. They might think I am influencing your choice." He is whispering, a tense expression replacing his easy smile.

Who is Luke referring to when he says "they?"

"I need more information. What should I choose?"

"Did you not just hear me? I can't tell you."

"At least tell me what category you are in." I am desperate. If I know which category he is in, I can follow him there. At least I will be able to find him if I need anything.

"I can't, I'm sorry." Luke looks away from me without another word and walks back to the circle of instructors.

When it is time, all of the initiates file into the building and line up at the edge of the room. Even though this is a conference room, it looks like a giant amphitheater. The seats are stacked in rows, one higher than the other, so everyone can see the stage in the middle of the room. There is a table on the stage covered in black, velvety cloth. On the table are two slips of paper, each with a pin on top of it. One piece of paper has a gold, cursive "I" pin laying on it. The other piece of paper has a gold, cursive "V" pin laying on top of it.

"Hello, ladies and gentlemen, and welcome to the Selection." The person talking is a short man around the age of 40. I recognize him as one of the city council members. "Our eighteen-year-olds will either choose Vigor or Intelligence. They must follow the guidelines in each section and live their life in line with their chosen category. By signing the contract on the left, they will pledge their life to a life of thinking and solving. They will be in Intelligence and will exemplify their mental strength in many areas of life. Then, they will take the "I" pin and wear it proudly through training.

By signing the contract on the right, they will pledge their life to a life of physicality and tactfulness. They will be in Vigor and will exemplify their physical strength in many areas of life. Then, they will take the "V" pin and wear it proudly through training.

We believe everyone requires both physical and mental prowess, although individuals may be more proficient in one than the other. Our goal is to hone our strengths for the ultimate good of society. Whichever pin you take, you must show and develop your strength in that area. Children, you are stepping into your role in society. Take all the time you need. The choice is yours."

One person after another steps up to the podium, deciding their fate with a simple signature. My palms are sweaty. What am I going to choose? Then, the first "S" is called. Five more people. Four. Will I be in Intelligence? Three more. Two. Will I be in Vigor? The man calls out, "Kiara Smith!"

Taking my time, I slowly walk down the aisle. The eyes of the entire crowd are on me, waiting to see what I decide. I could be smart or strong, a teacher or a protector. Follow in my parent's footsteps or make my own. During the physical test, I felt powerful, like I could do anything I set my mind to. Is that a sign?

Reaching for the black pen that is lying in front of me, I realize I want to feel that power again. I sign the Vigor contract and take the "V" pin.

"Miss Kiara Smith has chosen the Vigor path. Please walk through the right door." He gestures to a door at the right of the room. It has a big, golden "V" on it. Following his command, I walk toward it. *I just decided to start my path: to learn physical abilities and train my body instead of my mind. Did I make the right choice?*

As soon as I open the door, a crowd of people rushes to congratulate me. Looking around for a familiar face, I catch Clara's eye. We picked the same choice. A smile spreads across my face as I sigh with relief. I couldn't imagine going through training without her.

The crowd disperses, leaving me with Clara. "I see you picked the Vigor path," she says in an artificially serious tone. Her smile reaches her eyes, which are beaming with joy. She looks like she just won the lottery.

"You too, Ms. Larson." I give her a big hug. "When does training start?"

"It starts tomorrow. They give us one day to rest, and then they hit us with training."

"I'm glad we don't have to wait. I'd rather start sooner and get it over with."

After several minutes of waiting and several more students walking into this room, Luke opens the door and beckons for us to gather around him. "Good job everyone! You passed your tests and ended up here in Vigor. We welcome you. Training starts tomorrow. I assume you all know the location of the training facilities. I expect everyone to be in the physical training facility by 8:00 a.m. tomorrow. That's all for now, so goodbye." I figured he had chosen Brawn. Luke is incredibly smart, but he belongs here.

Relief washes over me as we leave the building. I have been worried for years about the Evaluation and the Selection, and it is finally over. Now, I just have to get through two months of training. Then, I can start my life.

CH∧PTER 8

WHEN I WAKE UP, the clock reads 7:30. I can't be late on the first day. As soon as I am dressed, I sprint downstairs, grab a piece of toast, and tell Mom and Jacob, "Bye."

The training facilities are about ten minutes from my house, so it doesn't take long to get there. I speed down the roads and quickly park my car. The Vigor and Intelligence buildings are right beside each other, both being tall, modern buildings with long glass windows. As I walk up to the building, I see my distorted reflection. My auburn hair glints in the window.

Yesterday, I didn't notice who had chosen Vigor. Looking around now, I see many familiar faces. Half of these people were on my sports teams or in my classes, but there are at least twenty-five people who I have never talked to before. I spot Clara in the crowd and run up to her. She gives me the biggest bear hug.

This will be a clean slate. New friends, new environment, new life. Of course, Clara will always be my best friend. That will never change.

When I catch sight of Luke, my heart skips a beat. During training, I must ignore him. I can't let my feelings get in the way of my progress. I came here for a reason, and I am going to come out on top. Luke looks at me and smiles. Hiding my feelings, I quickly look away and turn towards Clara.

There is only one room on the first floor. It is big and open, with tall ceilings, similar to a basketball gym. On one side of the room, punching bags line the walls. On the other side of the room, there are benches placed side by side. In the middle of the room, there are four fighting rings. Remembering back to the physical test, I was the only one who beat Luke in the ring.

Standing in the middle of one of the rings is a young man around the age of 30. All of us crowd around him, expecting him to speak.

"Welcome, trainees, to the Vigor facility. I am Matthew Carmen, and this is your training facility for the next two months. This is where you'll discover all physical jobs and eventually select your own. But first, you must learn about our ways. Your test administrators, Luke and Lora, will give you a tour of the building."

"All right, you heard the man. Let's start the tour," Luke yells. He leads the crowd to a set of metal doors.

As we walk, Luke and Lora explain each level of the building. The training facility is a lot bigger than it looks. The bottom floor is where most of the training takes place, and the second floor is full of classrooms. This is where all the textbook and intellectual learning happens. Although we chose a physical path, we still need to have knowledge about our jobs and what is going on in the world around us.

The third floor is primarily a workout floor. Each room has different exercises, from floor weights to equipment to aquatic training to sports. The next floor, which we will hardly ever use, is full of offices for all the trainers and staff. Finally, the top floor comprises dorms and lounging areas.

"That concludes our tour. Any questions?" Lora asks.

"Why do we need dorms?" a boy from the back of the crowd asks.

"In case you haven't heard from your parents or siblings, you will stay here over the weekdays for training and will be allowed to go home on certain weekends. Anything else?" Luke says.

"When does training start?" Clarisse asks.

Oh wow! I didn't know she chose Strength. "As soon as you walk downstairs, " I answer.

The crowd heads back to the elevators, but Luke quickly steps in front of us. "Rule #1: The elevators are prohibited during training. Before and after training sessions, feel free to use them. During training, you must always take the stairs. Go!"

Lora holds the door open as the crowd of trainees runs down the stairs. When we reach the bottom, we are all out of breath.

The man who stood in the middle of the ring when we arrived, Matthew Carmen, awaits us with three new people. "These are your trainers. You already know Luke and Lora. This is Kacy, the techniques trainer. Bryan over here specializes in a majority of the jobs, ultimately helping you learn your job to the best of your ability. Griffin primarily helps you train your body, similar to a personal trainer. He is a professional fighter, but he will also give you personal workouts and help with fitness.

"Lora is the smart one around here. She will finish out your education and prepare you to enter the world. Finally, Luke is the head of all the trainers. He oversees most things but also teaches a few jobs. There are a few more teachers under each instructor, but you will only meet the ones designated for you. Now, go pick a bunk and have the day off. Tomorrow starts your real training."

Clara and I rush up the stairs. We are one of the first people to reach the dorms. There are two dorm rooms, one for girls and one for boys. Each dorm room holds sixty twin beds stacked on top of each other, forming thirty bunk beds. Clara and I grab two bunk beds against the wall. We are close enough to the door to get out easily but not so close that we will hear everyone who leaves and enters the room. After settling in, we choose to sit on the top bunk, which belongs to Clara.

"I can't wait for training tomorrow. Are you excited, Kiara?" Clara asks. Her eyes are round with excitement, and she looks like she is absorbing every detail in this room.

"Yeah."

"And what about being trained by that scary guy Lu—" her sentence is cut off as Luke walks up to us.

My pulse quickens. *Remember, Kiara, ignore your feelings for him. It will make it easier in the long run.*

"Sorry to interrupt you, but can I borrow Kiara for a second?"

"Of course." Clara gives me a pointed look that tells me she hopes I survive. Then, she lays back on her bed as I head over to the door.

We walk back down to the first floor and out of the training facility. He leads me to a small building a couple of blocks from the Brawn and Brain facilities. It looks broken down, as if it has been out of use for several years. Luke leads me inside, and I am overwhelmed. On the outside, the building looks abandoned and dark. However, the inside holds new punching bags, tables, desks, fighting rings, heavy equipment, guns, and brand-new computers.

"Luke, what is this place?"

"This is the Amari training center. As head of training in the physical facility, it is my duty to find all the young Amari, get them trained and ready, and keep them hidden from the government. This is where they train and master their abilities. Only the Amari know about it."

"How come you know about it, Luke?"

He pauses for a second, debating whether he is going to say something. "I was entrusted to help the young Amari, like you."

Changing the subject before I can ask any more questions, he continues. "Kiara, allow me to elaborate. The Amari are a group of people with enhanced abilities that protect our world from evil threats in every country. They continue to grow stronger and expand their family. If a family has no blemishes and the Amari have not married a non-Amari, they pass down the abilities to all of their kids. If an Amari marries an outsider, then these abilities will only be passed down sporadically. The only way to ensure the abilities will be passed down is if two Amari marry."

A weight drops in my stomach as he continues to talk. Although I feel like I have accepted the fact that I am an Amari, it still comes as a shock to me. I am different from everyone else. I am physically and mentally enhanced. Are my parents Amari? Is Jacob? Will I always be different? The world starts spinning before me. Black spots dot the edge of my vision. I need to sit down.

Stumbling over to the nearest chair, I sit down with a thud. Luke quickly hands me a glass of water.

"Are you okay?"

"Yeah, I'm fine. I just realized I will never be a normal girl again. No big deal." I say the last sentence sarcastically.

"I know it's hard to accept, but all Amari have to at one point."

"That doesn't make me feel any better." I take a small sip of the water. "Is there anything else I need to know?"

"Well, you didn't let me finish. Every Amari is both enhanced in their physical abilities as well as their mental abilities. However, most people tend to be stronger in either one or the other. There are some Amari that are equally strong in both, though. They are very unique."

"What are you stronger in, Luke?" Maybe I'll catch him off guard, and he will slip up and say he is an Amari.

"Remember, I'm not Amari." He says this with a frown.

"Oh. Well, what about me? What is my strength?"

"You show signs of being equally strong in both. You are special." A moment of silence passes between us. I am unique.

"So, why are some stronger in one instead of the other? Why not just be strong in both?"

"A person's genetics only allow them to be stronger in one or the other. Unlike you, they are only lucky enough to be enhanced in one area." Concern fills Luke's eyes as he reads my facial expressions.

"So, on top of being different from normal people, I am also different from every other Amari."

"Yes." He looks me dead in the eyes and holds my gaze. "I know it's a lot to take in, but I'm here if you need anything."

"Thank you." Forcing a smile, I walk out of the building. Luke follows me as we walk back in silence.

Once we are back in the physical facility, I take the elevator up alone. Luke had to stay on the first floor and sort out the schedule for tomorrow. When I walk back into the dorm room, Clara is exactly where I left her, lying on her bed. There are clothes on top of my bed, most likely for our training tomorrow.

"Hey," I say to her, jumping on her bed.

"What? Why'd you wake me up? I was sleeping." Clara props herself up into a sitting position and rubs the sleep from her eyes. "What took you so long?"

"Well...um...Luke had to tell me something about, um, about tomorrow. And then I got dizzy because of..." I can't tell her about the Amari, "...because of the heat. Luke made sure I was fine and then brought me back here."

"Sure," she says in a skeptical voice. "It's time to go to bed. They told us lights need to be out at 10 p.m."

"All right." The lights shut off, and we all go to sleep.

CH/\PTER 9

THE FIRST WEEK of training flies by. During the week, we learn about all the different physical jobs and their training. The teaching category seems the most interesting. I could be a sports trainer or a teacher like Luke or an instructor. There are so many options.

Today, Matthew beckons all 100 trainees to gather around him. "Each of you has spent the week learning about each of the job categories. Now, you must pick a section that will alter your training courses in order to best suit you. Everyone in the category will be ranked by their training scores. If you fall below the minimum score by the end of training, well, let's just say you don't want to fall below the rankings.

"Also, there are only so many desirable jobs available in each category. I suggest you pick something you are good at because the top-scoring trainee will pick their job first, and the trainee ranked last will pick last. Keep that in mind. Of course, you can be promoted throughout the years, but it takes a lot of skill and hard work. I will call your names, and you will state which job category you want. First, Joshua Allen."

Matthew continues to call each trainee's name as I imagine what my life will look like in the near future. "Kiara Smith."

"Teaching category," I reply. It's crazy that those two words, my choice, can alter where I end up in life. Now that I think about it, the last few choices I have made have dramatically impacted my life.

"Each category has a designated instructor. That instructor is holding a sign with their category. Find them and follow them to your new classroom."

I scan the room for the "Teaching" instructor. Turns out, it's Luke. How convenient. Forcing a smile, I walk up to him. "So, you're my instructor?"

"What a coincidence." He winks at me. "I always end up training those who pick the Teaching category. Head up to Room 204. That's my room."

Following his direction, I journey upstairs to the second floor and find Room 204. When I walk in, I see Clara sitting at one of the desks. I had been so spaced out that I didn't even realize my best friend picked the same category as me. "Clara, you're in the teaching division, too?"

"Yeah! I can't believe you ended up here. Honestly, I thought you would take a job in the fighting category or something. After I picked my category, I completely zoned out, so I didn't even hear what you chose."

Drawing my attention away from Clara, I notice there are two boys sitting in front of her. I sit down at a desk next to her. Clara continues, "Anyway, this is Frank Ceagan and Alex Stone. They are both in the training division with us." She steals a glance at Alex; she must like him! I'll ask her about it later.

Luke walks into the room. "Hey guys! You are the trainees who have chosen the training category. There are eighteen of you now, and hopefully, eighteen of you will pass at the end. In order to pass, there is a certain score you must meet by the end of the year. Look over at this whiteboard." He points to a whiteboard on the left side of the room and continues, "I will update your rankings and scores every week so you will know if you are above or below the standard along with your rank. Understood?"

We all murmur in agreement.

"Every week, the minimum score will be updated. If you haven't passed the minimum, it's important to work hard next week and raise your score. After two weeks of being below the minimum, it is hard to get back up above it."

We all look at each other. Clara makes eye contact with me, communicating with her eyes. If either one of us falls below the line, we might end up being separated from each other. *That will not happen. I'll make sure of it.*

"There are two parts to this training. The first part will be physical training, toning your body and mind to do what you want it to do. If you can't train yourself, you can't train others. Now, head downstairs to the fighting rings. We start fighting now."

We sprint down the stairs to the fighting rings. Luke stands in the middle of one of them, waiting for all of us. He must have taken the elevator. "Each week, you will fight a fellow classmate. If you beat them, you will gain points and most likely move up in your ranks. If you lose, you may move down in the ranks, but you will still gain points if you have improved over the week.

"These fights, along with your progress in the classroom, will determine your rank and your score. Today, you will fight me so I can get a baseline of your skills. Now, line up on the punching bags. If you're not fighting, you're practicing. Cheap shots are banned, along with preying on the weak. Understood?"

We nod and line up on the punching bags. Since I am third in line, I have limited time to practice. This fight will be different. Luke will start off stronger, and he will be the same for girls and boys. I have to work for it. After punching at a bag a couple of times, I am called up. Luke pinned the two students in front of me with ease. How will he fight with me?

I step into the ring. Before I even look up, I feel a blow to the stomach. Immediately buckling, I hold my hands at the point of contact. "Thanks for the cheap shot. Aren't you supposed to be a nice teacher or something?"

"During training, I need to push you. Plus, that was not a cheap shot. Now get up and fight." His hands are in closed fists by his face. My face is already hot, and sweat is dripping down my neck. I guess I'll have to fight him hard. A fire ignites within me.

"Well, okay then, *trainer*, come fight me." Luke lunges at me, but I sidestep him. He's ready, though, and reels his elbow to my face. It misses by inches. Feeling annoyed, I pull my knee up and slam him in the stomach. Caught off guard, he staggers back.

"You want to play dirty?" Luke spits at me. I've never seen him like this before. There's a fire blazing in his eyes.

"You're the one who whipped your elbow at my face. I think I have the right to protect myself."

Despite thrusting my fist at his face, he ducks and catches my arm. Luke pins it against my back, but I kick him in the knee, making his knees buckle. I untangle my arm from his grasp and push him to the ground. Using most of his strength, he punches me in the stomach, but I ignore the pain. In return, I tackle him and hold his throat with one hand, tight enough to pin him down but not tight enough to hurt him. Putting my knees on his arms so he can't hit me, I pull my arm back as if I am about to punch him.

"Are we done?" I plea.

"Only if you can punch me."

"But I don't want to punch someone I like." Too late. The words came out before I could stop them. My face turns bright red, and heat rushes into my cheeks. Why does this always happen? First during the Evaluation, now here.

Luke blushes a little bit but ignores what I just admitted. "You must train your mind to get over anything, even if it goes against the thing you like." At the word "like" he stares me dead in the eyes. "Now punch me."

I can't. I won't punch him. But I have to. Taking a deep breath and closing my eyes, I punch Luke in the nose. His nose pops and then starts to bleed. "Oh my gosh. I can't believe I just punched you. Are you okay?"

"I'm fine. It's just a nosebleed." Tears well up in my eyes, but I suppress them. There is no way that I am going to cry. Not here, not now. His face turns serious. "Stay after this session. I need to talk to you." Luke walks out of the ring and dabs his nose with a paper towel. After writing a few notes about our fight, he calls the next person into the ring.

I walk out of the ring feeling awful. *Why does he need to talk to me? What did I do wrong? His face looked so serious. Was it because I punched him? This can't be good.*

Alex, who was the first person to fight Luke, beckons me to come sit down. "How was your fight, Alex?"

"I got punched a lot, but it was fine. You beat him, though. Honestly, you made it look so easy."

"Trust me, it was harder than it looked. Plus, I'll have a few bruises on my side."

Eventually, Luke finishes with all the trainees. He dismisses us for the day so that he can record the data from our fights. Everyone walks back up to the dorms or the workout rooms. Since Luke wanted me to wait for him, I tell Alex, Frank, and Clara to go up without me.

Luke jogs up to me from the benches. His nose has stopped bleeding and is now a bright shade of red.

"Hey. What did you need to talk to me about?"

"Well, I was just wondering," he looks down at his feet and scratches the back of his neck, "if you wanted to hang out with me tonight. I have something I think you might like." His face turns pink.

"Are you asking me out on a date?"

Luke turns a brighter shade of red. "Do you want it to be a date?"

With a big grin on my face, I look up at him. "Yes. When do you want to meet up?"

"Can you meet me down here at 6:00?"

"Yeah." My smile spreads wider across my face, and I stare deep into his eyes. I didn't notice it before, but his right eye has little specks of orange in it. Snapping myself out of this sudden daze, I pull myself away from Luke. While I don't want to leave him, it would seem weird if I spent a long time down here with my instructor. "See you then."

When I walk back up to the lounging areas, I see Clara sitting on a couch alone with Alex and Frank on the neighboring couch. I can't stop smiling, but I must look like everything is normal. Sliding the smile off of my face, I plop down next to Clara.

"What was that about?" she asks in a sarcastic tone.

"Luke just needed to talk to me about..." *think, Kiara, think,* "... about my fight. Apparently, I fought well." I hate lying to my friends, but I don't want to explain this weird relationship in mixed company. Even if it doesn't turn into something, I don't want them to know about it before I am certain where this will lead.

"No, duh," Frank says. "You knocked him out in less than five minutes."

"Are you sure you've never fought before?" Alex asks. A hint of jealousy grips his tone, so I quickly reply.

"I'm sure. It's probably just beginner's luck." There's a moment of silence as we all guess why I am such a good fighter.

"Anyway, what are y'all going to do after training?" Clara always knows how to release tension in a room. To show my gratitude, I gently nudge her elbow.

"I'm going to get a house and never come back here," Alex says.

"What's so bad about this?" Clara asks.

"Training is just not fun. I constantly feel like I have to prove myself and get a good ranking. It's been one day, and I am already stressed out."

"Fair enough," Frank says. Pausing for a moment, he adds, "I think I'm going to ask out that girl, Sarah."

"No offense, but I think she's a bit out of your league, Frank."

"Alex, don't be mean." Clara turns to Frank and puts on a serious face. "You two would be a cute couple."

Nodding, I say, "I agree. When are you going to do it?"

"How are you going to do it?" Clara adds.

"Y'all are so nosy. I'm not going to tell you. It will probably be soon, though."

"Fine. We won't ask the love-sick man any more questions." A grin spreads across Alex's face as Frank punches him.

We carry on with our conversation, talking about random things and laughing at stupid jokes.

Three hours pass by, and I realize I have a date in 30 minutes. After pulling my hair out of my ponytail, I let it fall across my shoulders and back. Then, I unzip my jacket a bit and get up from the couch.

"Where are you going?" Clara asks.

I can't tell her about Luke. "Just to walk around. I need some fresh air, but I'll be back in a little while, okay?"

Clara gets up from the couch and stares me dead in the eyes. "Where are you actually going?"

Meeting her stare, I try to act casual. "I'm just going out for a walk. It's been a long day, and I'm tired from the fight."

"The fight that you won?" she asks skeptically.

"Clara, I'll be back in a few hours. Please, just let me have some time alone."

"Okay," she says warily. "Have fun on your so-called walk, but don't think I don't know you're lying. I'll be waiting." Clara then turns to Alex and Frank, accepting that I won't give in, and carries on with their conversation.

Guilt hangs over me as I rush downstairs. I hate lying to Clara, but I think it was the right thing to do for the time being. When I reach the first floor, Luke is waiting by one of the fighting rings.

"You look nice." He smiles at me. "Are you ready?"

"Yes." Luke grabs my hand and leads me out the door. My hand fills with electricity.

We sit in silence as he drives us to a hotel about five minutes from the training facilities. I tense up; I don't want this date to go down the wrong path.

Luke looks over at me. My hands are clenched so tight that my knuckles are white, and I am sitting as straight as a pole. He puts it together. "Don't worry, I'm not that shallow. I want to take you to the top of the building." *Luke would never do something like that, especially on a first date.* Why would I even think that? Sensing my embarrassment, he grabs my hand and squeezes it, releasing my anxiety into the air.

When we reach the hotel, we park the car and take the elevator to the top floor. As soon as the elevator doors open, I feel a powerful gust of wind hit me. Stumbling back a few steps, I catch myself and walk out with Luke. He guides me to the edge of the roof, and we sit down side-by-side. Even though it is summer, shivers run down my body from the wind.

"So, what do you think?"

The view overwhelms me. Colorful lights cover the entire city. Every color imaginable is in this beautiful landscape. There are strands of lights outlining each building in the city, making a colorful silhouette for each one. Some buildings have gradients, others contain stark contrasts of yellow and red or purple and green. A sea of color fills my view, and the beauty overwhelms me. I feel how small we are in this giant world. We are just specks in a world full of color and movement. "It's beautiful."

"Sometimes, I come up here at night to enjoy the beauty of our city. It's my escape from everything around me." We stare into the landscape of color for what feels like hours, taking in the flashing lights and colorful city.

"Luke, why did you choose Vigor?" He is incredibly smart, but also strong. Luke could just as easily be in Intelligence. Even though he is not an Amari, I wonder if he is like me: performing excellently in both categories.

"Why do you think?"

"You are an incredibly strong man, and your Evaluation told you to choose Vigor?"

"Ding, ding, ding." He smiles at me.

"Well, I think you are really smart."

A moment of silence passes. Then, he leans over and whispers into my ear, "Can I kiss you?"

A grin spreads over my face. My heart races, and my pulse quickens. Before I can give it a second thought, I turn toward him and press my lips to his. Energy buzzes throughout me. Any coldness leaves my body instantly. I wrap my arms around his neck, and he places his hands on my back. A thrill runs through my body. His lips brush against mine. Our foreheads are pressed together.

These moments feel like an eternity. His arms wrap around me, and I lean my head against his shoulder. Luke begins playing with a lock of my hair. We stare out into the city's lights. The colorful glow of the city still entrances me. This has been the best night I have had in a long time. Reluctantly, I glance at my watch, which reads 9:00. We have been sitting on this ledge for three hours. I don't want this to end, but I say, "We should probably head back."

"Okay," he whispers into my hair. Luke kisses the side of my head and stands up. We walk back to the car, hand-in-hand. I can't stop smiling. While walking, I look up at him and notice a grin on his face. He enjoyed it just as much as I did.

We walk back through the training facility and take the elevator to the fifth floor. When the doors open, I smile up at him and sneak back into the girls' dorm room. I hear heavy breaths and faint snores. Everyone is asleep. Trying not to make too much noise, I climb into my bed.

My hand is still warm from holding Luke's hand. I smile. Luke is at the front of my mind as I slowly drift off to sleep.

CH/\PTER 10

"HERE'S A BREAKDOWN of what the next two months will look like. We will train your bodies during the first month and focus on your intellect in the second month." It has been two days since I went out with Luke. His nose is still a light shade of yellow and green from our fight, and other bruises dot his skin. Despite the bruises, he has seemed lighter and happier since our date. He smiles more and occasionally glances towards me. "There are eighteen jobs available for you. If you do not meet the standard, you will not get a job. Work hard. Train hard. That is your motto for the next two months. If you do that, then you will succeed."

We all walk down to the fighting rings and wait for further instructions. Luke beckons us over to the benches, where we all take a seat. "Like I said last week, you will fight each other in order to determine both your improvement and your physical standing with the other trainees. If you win, you move up in the rankings. If you lose, you move down. Either way, you should still gain some points as long as you have improved." Luke pauses for a second. "Your opponents are on the whiteboard behind me. Kiara, you are up first with Paul."

Paul is one of the strongest fighters here. He is tall and lean but pure muscle. Clara told me that he has been fighting since he could walk, so this will be a tough match. Pumping myself up, I prepare my body for the bruises and punches I am about to receive. Once we are both in the ring, we put our hands up by our faces and begin the fight.

Immediately, I see a blur and feel a sharp pain in my ribs. A sly smile slides across Paul's face. What just happened? I try to punch his face, but he deflects my fist and strikes my jaw. Then, I try to kick him, but Paul catches my foot and pulls me toward him. With that same smile still plastered across his face, he wraps his hands around my waist and flips me on my back. Panic hits me; I have to get back up. Paul will start kicking, and that is ten times worse than being punched. I stumble to my feet.

"Have you had enough, sweetheart?" His voice is cool, like a panther stalking its prey.

"You wish." My heart is racing. *This is much harder than I anticipated.*

"Suit yourself." Paul lunges at me, grabbing my neck and putting me in a chokehold. After a few seconds filled with me gasping for air, he then punches me in the gut and slaps my ear. I hear ringing, and the room starts to spin. Luke is shaking his head in the corner.

Reorienting myself, I ram my elbow into his side, but he responds with a jab to my nose. Something wet drips over my lips: blood.

"Are we done here? I'm bored." What a sick man.

"Yeah." Luke waves Paul away and walks back to his clipboard.

Paul glances over at me. "I thought you were good at fighting. Guess not." With a smirk on his face, he walks out of the ring. Heat rises in my cheeks. Everyone just saw me lose to Paul. I got beat up like a rag doll, like a worthless piece of garbage.

"Luke, why did you stop the fight?" Fury rises in me as I storm over to him. I try to keep my voice even despite my sudden rage. "I still could have won. I could have come back."

"Kiara, let's not do this in front of everyone. I stopped the fight before anything bad happened. Can you just go sit down?"

"No, I can't just go sit down. Everyone just saw me get beat like a doll, and then you stopped the fight before I could even respond. How would that make you feel?"

"I'm sorry, but I just don't want you to get hurt."

"Luke, I think you need to remember that I am in Brawn for a reason. I can handle this." Without another word, I walk out of the ring just as the next pair prepares to fight. No one will ever beat me like that again. That was humiliating and agonizing. And to think Luke stopped the fight before I could even retaliate. How weak does he think I am?

My temper slowly cools as the rest of the groups fight. My nose has stopped bleeding, and my head no longer pounds. Paul is sitting in the corner with a smirk on his face. His sly smile makes me want to strangle him, but I control the urge.

"Good job, everyone. We'll continue training tomorrow. Get a good night's sleep." Luke walks away from us, not even looking in my direction. He is ashamed of me; I am sure of it. Honestly, I wouldn't blame him. After being known as the best fighter in the group, he has to stop the fight early in order to prevent me from getting hurt. How pathetic is that?

Once I grab an ice pack from the cooler, I slowly climb up the girls' dorm room. This is by far the worst day of training. Making it clear that I am in no mood to talk, I head straight to my bed. Clara, sensing my irritation, gives me some time alone. Feeling both dejected and humiliated, I silently lie on my bed, pretending to sleep as I ice my wounds.

After everyone is asleep, I quietly climb out of my bed. Still wearing the clothes from today, I walk downstairs to the punching bags. I guide myself through the dark area to the first punching bag I find. I won't allow myself to be beaten up in the same way again. I refuse to relive that humiliation and frustration. Not only would I lose all my points, but I would drop in the rankings.

With a firm resolve in my mind, I hit the first punching bag. Adjusting my stance, I hit it again, this time stronger. I kick the punching bag with all of my might, step back, and attack it again. In order to be a successful fighter, I must learn to use my body in the best way possible. I am not the strongest puncher, but my kicks are deadly. If I can just kick my opponent to his knees, then I can pin him to the ground and win the fight.

"What are you doing?"

Startled, I ask, "Who's there?"

"It's just me." He pauses for a second. "Luke."

"What are you doing here?" My tone reflects my irritation with him.

"I couldn't sleep, so I thought I might work on my fighting." His footsteps echo in the room.

Turning back toward the punching bag, I say, "I'm working on fighting right now, so you will just have to come back another time."

Luke continues walking toward me as I kick the punching bag. "How are you feeling after your fight?"

"How do you think? Embarrassed, dejected, and like a loser. It didn't help that you just stood there shaking your head the whole time. And to make it worse, you ended the fight early. How do you think that makes me feel?"

"What was I supposed to do, Kiara?" Luke sounds like he is accusing me, like he is trying to justify his own actions. "You were being punched left and right. Your face was bloody, but there was no way I was going to stop the fight by saying, 'That's enough. She needs a break.' How would that make you feel? Like an incapable fighter who can't do anything. All I was trying to do was look out for you. I wanted it to feel more like a treaty than a surrender."

My head drops. "Whatever. I was going to lose, anyway." I half-heartedly kick the punching bag again, but it barely moves.

There is a long, heavy silence between us as Luke searches for the right words. "Do you want help training?" Hope fills his voice. I can barely make out his face in the dark, but I can tell he is looking at me.

"I don't need your help."

"I know you don't need it, but do you want it?" Luke waits in hopeful anticipation.

In reality, I desperately want and need Luke's help. My pride has blinded me in the past, but I need to open my eyes and realize that Luke wants what is best for me. "Yes." I drop my hands and wait for him to walk over to me.

"So, you have a firm foot. Your punches are okay. Once you get stronger, they will break a nose. As for chokeholds, that seems to be your weakness. You beat me by elbowing my stomach, but Paul tied your hands back. The thing is, act calm. Fake it until you make it. If you are calm, then your opponent will loosen their grip on you. If they don't, then headbutt them. It may hurt you, but it will hurt them worse. Practice on me, but please don't actually hit me."

Luke walks over to me and puts his elbow under my chin. I take a few deep breaths, remembering back to my fight. Paul's mouth was right behind my head. Luke is taller, so I will most likely hit his chin. Following his instruction, I pull my head back and hit bone. I refuse to show any signs of my headache despite the impact. I have to act tough.

Luke groans with pain. "I said go easy on me."

"That is payback for making me feel like a helpless nobody today." I pause for a second, then turn around and gently press my lips to his chin. "And that's for helping me."

A smile slides across his face, and he temporarily forgets his pain. "Glad to be of service. Now, go back to bed. You need rest. We'll work on this later, maybe not in the middle of the night."

"Whatever you say, Luke." Suddenly becoming exhausted, I wander back to the elevator. As the doors close, I hear the faint sound of him hitting the punching bag.

CHAPTER 11

THROUGHOUT THE NEXT two weeks, we work out and continue fighting. Every night, Luke helps me train and work on my fighting skills. So, I successfully win both of my fights against Frank and a girl named Maggie. Fighting Frank was tough. Besides being one of my best friends, he is an incredibly skilled fighter. Unlike Maggie, he knows how to throw a punch. I tried to kick him a couple of times, but Frank just deflected me.

Honestly, the only reason I won was because Frank messed up when he lunged at me. I was able to grab him and push him to the ground. From there, I pinned his hands and knees. Both of us still have rankings above the minimum, so it wasn't a big deal that he lost. The best reward was having bragging rights over him for a week.

Our next fight is today. "Who do you think our opponents are this week?" Clara whispers into my ear.

"It's probably going to be Alex and Paul." Paul is second under me. After our fight, he lost to one of the lower-ranked trainees. Paul dropped a few ranks because of the loss but has recovered. However, he can't stand that I am above him in the ranks.

"You really think I'm up against Alex? There is no way that I will win that fight." Lines of worry etch Clara's face.

"What are you talking about, Clara? You are an amazing fighter. I'm just afraid that if I go against Paul again, he is going to use illegal shots in order to win."

"That's not even a question. He wants payback." We both eye Paul, who is flirting with Maggie. I wonder why he is talking to one of the weaker trainees. Is he trying to charm her into doing something for him? The thought sends a chill through me.

"Kiara! You're up!" Luke calls me into the ring.

Mentally preparing myself for what's ahead, I step into the ring and look over at Luke. We haven't had a real conversation since the night I lost to Paul. He has trained me most nights, but we don't really talk then. Luke just gives me pointers and then goes to bed. I hope that will change soon.

"Luke, who is my opponent?" I ask. My question is answered when Griffin, the 200-pound professional fighter and workout trainer, steps into the ring. Confused and upset, I walk over to Luke while Griffin is wrapping his hands in tape. "This is not fair. I won't beat Griffin."

"Kiara," he looks me dead in the eyes, "you need to learn to lose. Trust me on this; you will thank me later. Plus, you will become a better fighter if you fight people who are above your skill level. Good luck." Remorse fills his eyes.

"Is this even legal?" I am freaking out. I don't want to get hurt, to lose, to feel the impending pain. Terror and anxiety grip my mind.

Luke drops his eyes to the floor. "I'm sorry. I had no choice." Turning his back on me, he walks out of the ring. "Fight!"

Griffin steps toward me. How will I beat a monster like him? He throws a punch at my side. Evading the jab, I move to the left, stepping right into his next punch. My side is throbbing. Using all of my force, I kick him in the side, but he doesn't even flinch. Griffin adjusts his stance as if he is going to kick me. I ready myself for the kick, but I am knocked back when he spins around and elbows me in the side.

Feeling irritated, I punch him in the face, only to be punched right back. I won't give up. There has to be a weak spot. The world is spinning in front of me. Everyone is watching. I must win. Trying to catch him off guard, I spin around and thrust my leg into his side. Griffin catches it and flips me onto my back. I am about to be pinned.

There is no weak spot. I will not win. Using my remaining strength, I slide away from him, but I am not fast enough. This is definitely going to hurt. Hands covering his face, one more punch to the side of my head knocks me out cold.

I feel something soft beneath my head. When I open my eyes, I realize that I am lying in a white bed in a hospital room. Clara leans over me with a pale face. "You look pale, Clara. Are you all right?"

"Better question, are you all right? Griffin hit you so hard. Hold on. Let me get the nurse." Clara leaves the room and brings back a girl holding a clipboard a few seconds later. She looks young, in her early twenties. "This is your nurse. Her name is Candice."

"Hello." I nod at the nurse. "How long until I'm out of this bed? I need to get back to training."

"Don't worry, Kiara," she says. "You will be out of here in a couple of hours. We just need to make sure that the swelling goes down and that you don't have any bruised ribs. You have a black eye and a few bruises on your abdomen. Any questions? How are you feeling?"

"Like I got knocked out by a 200-pound dude. But I'm fine, thanks."

"Okay. Just call if you need anything." Candice leaves the room, followed by Clara, who insists that I get some rest.

After a few minutes, Luke walks into the room. A surge of anger rises in me. Luke put me here. He let me get beat up. "You let him hit me like that. In front of everyone, too. You knew I would lose."

His eyes look pained and upset like he can't take the accusatory comments. "Please don't be angry. I needed you to lose. You've been on a winning streak, and that is strange for someone with no experience. You only lost to Paul because he has a powerful punch. Ms. Cassini called before the fight, asking me to take a closer look at you. She has been watching you. I can't lose you to someone like her."

"That doesn't justify anything." I try to cross my arms, but pain shoots through my torso. So, I just leave them resting at my side.

"I'm just trying to protect you. What will all the leaders think when a girl with no experience beats every opponent? Huh? They might be a little confused and think that you are special. Just like Ms. Cassini, they'll probably conclude that you are an Amari."

"I don't need your protection." My voice is even as my increasing anger boils inside of me. "I don't need you to make me look weak. For most of my life, I've been known as a weak girl from Intelligence. Imagine people mocking you because your parents are from Brain, but your best friend is a Brawn. I don't want to be the joke, not now. Honestly, I thought you wanted me to succeed in training, not make me look like a weak eighteen-year-old girl."

My voice slowly gets louder, and I am almost yelling. Why would the leaders even care about my success? Compared to everything going on around me, I am just a random trainee who happens to be a good fighter.

Luke's voice rises, matching my intensity. "What's going to happen when the leaders conclude you are an Amari? You're dead." His eyes are glistening. "I just don't want to lose you."

"I don't need your help." But I do. I don't really know what I am or what all of this means. Tears are brimming in my eyes. "Luke,

I'm scared. What's going to happen to me? I don't want to be an Amari."

"Kiara, I know you're scared. It's okay. Always know that I care about you, and I will never let them hurt you; I won't let them hurt anyone. Not again."

"Not again?" Who did he lose? "What happened?"

Catching himself, he quickly puts on a blank face. "Umm, not here. I'll tell you later, I promise. And Kiara, I'm sorry. Will you please forgive me?" Luke looks deep into my eyes, searching for something, probably forgiveness. His eyes tilt down like he is worried for me, and he doesn't know what to do.

"Yes." I glance down at my hands, attempting to appear casual. "I'm sorry, too. Lately, I have been so stressed out with training and all the fighting. Plus, we haven't hung out since the date. What am I supposed to think after that? What did I do wrong?"

Silence fills the air for a few moments. "I wish we were together, but I don't want the others to think I am biased towards you. If you are free tonight, I have something I want to show you. Do you think you will be able to come?"

"I'll convince the nurses." His voice lightens like he feels comfortable again. His eyes are still glistening, but I see a slight grin at the corner of his mouth. Satisfied that I am okay, Luke leaves me to rest as I anticipate our upcoming date.

A few hours pass. I am alone, despite the occasional nurses who come in to check on me. Once I am cleared to leave the hospital in the afternoon, I slowly walk back to the training facilities. Luke stands in front of the physical training facility, talking to Lora.

"Hey, am I interrupting?"

"No, you're fine, Kiara." Luke looks at me as if scanning to see all of my injuries.

"I'm glad you're out of the hospital. Luke told me you took a beating in the ring today," Lora says to me.

I smile and nod at her. "Yeah. It hurts to move, but I'm getting through it."

"Lora, I'll talk to you later," Luke says. He gives her a side glance as if telling her something in a secret code.

Lora smiles at Luke and walks off, leaving Luke and me together. "Ready?" Touching my side, he says, "Does this hurt?"

"Just a little." I giggle at his concern for me and grab his hand. We walk a few yards, and then I stop and turn towards him. Something has been gnawing at my mind since I saw Luke with Lora, and I need to confront him before we move any further.

Confused, he asks, "You all right?"

"Luke, this might just be me, but are you and Lora ... have you two ever ..." I can't spit it out. "Are you two dating? Because if you are, I will not continue with whatever this is." I point at us. As much as I love being with Luke, I will never be with a guy who is secretly dating another girl.

Hurt fills his eyes as he looks away. "I'm not dating her, Kiara. I chose you, didn't I? Lora has just helped me through some tough times; she is like a sister to me."

"Oh, I'm sorry." My eyes drop to my feet, and heat rises in my cheeks. We stand there for a few awkward seconds. I don't know what to say.

Luke grabs my hand and says, "I understand your concern, but I would never betray you, okay?" Blush fills my cheeks from the compliment. Taking his hand in mine, I give him a heartfelt smile as we continue walking down the street.

We turn on the lights when we reach the Amari training facility. Luke leads me to a table on the left side of the room holding a piece of machinery with a bunch of wires attached to it. Next, he begins connecting himself to the wires.

"Luke, what is this?"

"It's a lie detector. You can ask me anything, and the small light right here will turn red if I lie," he says while pointing to a small light near the edge of the machine.

"Why would you let me, of all people, ask you anything?"

Luke stops hooking the wires up to himself and stares me dead in the eyes. "Because I trust you, and I don't want to keep secrets from you. I am willing to let you see my weaknesses." Without another word, he sits down in a chair and looks up at me. "Start off with something that you know is true."

"Okay. What is your name?"

"Luke Johnson."

"How old are you?"

"20."

"Will you answer every question to the best of your ability?"

"Yes." The light doesn't turn red. Luke will answer every question truthfully. Grateful for his trust and vulnerability, I give him a warm smile.

"What is your greatest fear?"

At this, he shifts in his chair. Luke's face is filled with discomfort, as if he doesn't want to answer the question. "Being the cause of a loved one's death."

A moment of silence passes between us, so I try to lighten it up by asking easier questions. "Are you afraid of spiders?"

"No."

"Snakes?"

"No."

"Are you claustrophobic?"

"Yes."

"Really? I didn't know that."

He grits his teeth, and his face turns bright red. "Well, now you do."

"What is something I don't know about you?"

"I was ranked first in Vigor training. I was in the training category, just like you, and I achieved the top ranking."

"That's amazing, Luke." Wow. He was first. "Oh! Have you ever dated anyone else?"

"Nope. Just you." Luke looks slightly embarrassed by this.

"If it makes you feel any better, I've only dated you."

He smiles at the comment. "Any more questions?"

"Do you love me?" While it is a very personal question, I want to know the answer. I want to make sure that we feel the same way about each other and that this won't be a one-sided relationship.

Luke shifts again and blankly stares at the ground. Then, looking up at me, he says, "Yes, Kiara, I love you so much. I love your playful grin and how you make others feel so loved. I love how ambitious and talented you are. Most of all, I love your deep blue eyes; they entrance me. They are as mysterious as the ocean, yet as bright as diamonds."

The light doesn't turn red; Luke is telling the truth. Heat rises in my cheeks, and a grin spreads across my face. An overwhelming sense of respect and love overcomes me as I realize just how much Luke loves me.

"That really means a lot, Luke. I love you, too." Luke holds my gaze for what feels like an eternity, his deep blue eyes searching mine. After a few moments, I drop my eyes to the floor and recollect myself. Then, I ask, "Do you trust me?"

"Yes."

My smile grows wider. "Just so you know, I would trust you with my life," Luke responds with a grin. A question then pops into my head, one he has avoided since the first time I asked him. "Are you an Amari?"

This question seems to make him even more uncomfortable, like he is giving up something he has tried to hide for so long. His knuckles turn white as he grabs the side of the chair. "Yes." It is a simple, little word, barely audible over the humming of the machine. I was right; he is an Amari.

"Why do you want to conceal it? You have tried so hard to keep it from me. If you trust me, why wouldn't you just tell me?"

"I—" he begins. "My best friend was an Amari. A couple of years ago, he was held for ransom by this small terrorist group. The government didn't give him a second glance solely because he was an Amari. So, I tried to save him, but I couldn't. I was stabbed in the side, barely missing my lungs. My friend was killed." Luke pauses for a moment, collecting his thoughts and calming himself down.

His eyes are glistening, but he tries to hide it. "I don't trust many people, or even open up around them for that matter. I have shown no one the scar, either. Lora was the only one, besides my parents, who knew about the whole incident and helped me through my loss."

Once he finishes, I stand there in awe, letting the silence hang between us. Luke just admitted something so personal that only three other people know about it. "That's also why I want to keep you safe. I couldn't bear it if I lost someone else, especially you." The realization hits me: all he wanted to do was save me from the fate of his best friend.

Luke's attempt at a carefree smile fails. As he pecks the wires off one by one, I make my way over to him. Standing up slowly, a look of uncertainty and embarrassment crosses his face. "So, what do you think?"

All I can do is stare up at him. Luke is the bravest and most selfless person I have ever met. He risked his life to save a loved one. And he trusted me to keep his secret. "Wow." I wrap him in my arms and whisper in his ear, "You're so strong, you know that?"

I feel him smile on my shoulder. We stand there, wrapped in each other's arms, for several minutes.

CHAPTER 12

AFTER SPILLING his secrets, he seems lighter—like he doesn't have an enormous weight on his shoulders. We both walk to the door of the Amari training facility, deciding it is time to head back. "You go ahead and walk back to the physical facility. I'll catch up. I just have to sort a few things out here."

"What are you working on?" Sometimes, my curiosity takes the best of me.

"Oh, just something for the Amari leaders. No big deal."

"Can you finish it another night?"

"I really wish I could, but they told me I have to finish it tonight. It has taken a long time to put together, and they want it done as soon as possible."

"Well, what is it?"

Luke hesitates for a second. "I want to tell you, but I can't. Something about being 'top secret.'" I look at him with skeptical eyes as he says, "Don't worry, I'll be quick."

"Are you sure you don't want me to wait for you?" I don't mind walking alone; walks at night are peaceful and relaxing. However, I don't want to leave him here. A part of me wants to walk at night with him, hand in hand, without a care in the world.

"Go ahead. It'll take me a few minutes, but I promise to sprint over when I'm done." Luke winks at me and then turns to one of the computers.

"Okay. Should I wait for you in front of the physical training facility?"

"Yeah." Giving me a quick smile, he starts typing on the computer in front of him. "Don't worry. I'll finish this as quickly as I can."

Satisfied with his answer, I open the door and start walking back to the training facility. The cool breeze sends a chill through my body. The night air is refreshing against my bruised skin. There is a sea of stars above me. Many of the constellations shimmer in the sky despite the light pollution from our city. Orion's belt and the Little Dipper hang above our city, precisely like the nights I used to stargaze with my mom.

About halfway back to the facility, I hear footsteps behind me. Turning around, I yell into the darkness, "Luke, that was fast. What did you do?" No one answers. That's strange. Maybe it was just my imagination. I keep walking.

Out of nowhere, a hand covers my mouth. I try to scream, but the hand suppresses my voice. Two more hands grab my arms and pull them behind my back. A rope slides around them and tightens. I keep screaming. Tears well up in my eyes. I can't move my arms; I am alone. No one can hear me, but I keep screaming. A blindfold covers my eyes. I try to kick, but someone is holding my feet; I am being carried. My screams are muffled as the hand persistently covers my mouth, leaving me hoarse. I hear a door open and close.

I make an effort to regulate my breathing, feeling ashamed for being taken by surprise. After a month of training and fighting, I should be prepared for this. At least three guys are carrying me, two holding my body and one covering my mouth. With all of my bruises, I will probably only be able to fight off two. There could be more men in this new room. How many will I have to fight off? Can I fight them all?

They drop my feet, and I stumble to a standing position. My abdomen aches from my previous bruises, but I try to ignore the pain. A deep, rough voice says, "Take her blindfold off." The cloth slips off my eyes. I don't know where I am. Tears streak my face. The man with the deep voice turns to me. My hands are still tied behind my back, and a hand covers my mouth. "Where is it? Where are the papers?"

The man removes his hand from my mouth. I shake my head and try to say, "What papers?" Yelling so much makes my voice croak. The guy behind me slaps the side of my head. My ears start ringing.

"I won't ask you again. Where are the Amari papers?"

"I—I don't know what you're talking about?" What does he know about the Amari? Why is he asking me about random papers? I didn't do anything wrong. My eyes are blurry with tears. Someone punches me in the gut and my body buckles. That's going to hurt tomorrow.

"Tell me now!"

I'm silent. Someone kicks me in the side, and I groan. My ribs throb. My head pounds. What do they want?

The man moves over to a short man standing in the corner. He whispers something that I can barely make out. "She's not responding to pain. What should we do?"

Pride wells up in my chest. I have stumped my kidnappers.

The short man walks up to me and looks me up and down as if he is scanning me for weaknesses. "What is your name, darling?" His voice is as cold as ice.

I will not tell him my real name. What should I say? "Olivia."

"Olivia, have you ever heard of the Amari?"

I have to play dumb. This man will kill me if I know about them. This is exactly what Luke was trying to protect me from. "No." I mean to say it louder, but it comes out as a whisper.

"Stop playing dumb with me, girl. I know you know all about them. I will get this information; you decide how. The easy way or the hard way?"

I keep my mouth shut; I don't want to say the wrong thing.

"The hard way it is. Keep beating her. She'll let it slip eventually." My heart pounds even faster. Terror rises in my gut. What will they do to me? Blows barrage my head. A man with black, greasy hair, who is holding a knife, walks up to me and kicks me in the side. Something wet drips down the side of my head. It is warm and has a red tint. Where am I bleeding?

The short man's face furrows with frustration as he yells, "Where are the documents?" I am silent. If I don't know what they are talking about, how can I answer the question?

Another blow to my head. My vision blurs, and tears fill my eyes. My head is throbbing, and I am doubled over in pain after being kicked in the stomach. My knees buckle, and I am kneeling on the ground. My hands strain against the rope, but I can't break it. I feel more bruises forming on my side, and I am sure a welt is already on my head.

The man with the greasy hair holds the knife to my throat as the short man yells at me. "I won't ask again. Where are the Amari papers?"

"I don't know!" I scream at him. My voice sounds distorted, a mix of a scream and a sob filled with pain. I feel the blade push into my skin. I don't want to die.

Suddenly, the man holding the knife falls to the ground. A black blur barrages him with blows. The rest of my kidnappers lunge at the blur. I try to focus on his face. Who is it?

I'm hit on the back of my head by the man who was holding me, and then he lets go to join the fight. One after another, my kidnappers fall to the ground. I become dizzy. My vision is dotted with black spots. The world spins in front of me. I slump to the floor. Just before I pass out, I see my rescuer. Brown hair and blue eyes. It's Luke.

When I open my eyes, I see Luke sitting in a chair across from me. Luke's eyebrows are crumpled, and a crease appears on his forehead. His eyes meet mine. Luke gets up from his chair, walks over to me, and kneels by my head. "How are you feeling?"

I meet his gaze and try to smile, but my head feels like it is splitting. A welt forms at the back of my head. "Not good."

Luke brings his hand to my face and wipes a tear away that I didn't even know was there. "Well, you have a welt on your head, and more bruises on your arms and face are coming out. You have a cut on your head that I already cleaned, and the bruises on your ribs from the fight with Griffin have already turned a deeper shade of red."

When I attempt to sit up, a sudden, intense pain shoots through my side. My ribs feel like fire. I groan in pain as I stabilize myself. "Everything hurts, Luke, and I was so scared. I had no idea what they were talking about." Panic and anxiety overwhelm me as I realize what just happened. Tears fall from my eyes as I process the attack.

"It's okay. I'm here now. We are safe." Luke grabs my hand and squeezes it. "I know it hurts, but you will get through this."

I focus on my breathing, trying to calm myself down. "They asked me about these Amari documents. They kept beating me because I wouldn't answer them, but I had no idea what they were talking about."

"Don't worry about it." He averts his eyes from mine; he's hiding something from me.

"Luke, I don't think you understand how important this is. Those guys were ready to beat me to death for those documents. I need to know what they are."

Luke tenses at the word "death" and looks back at me, his eyes full of worry. His knuckles are split from the fight, and he has a bruise just under his right eye. "Those documents they wanted are full of lists. It was what I was finishing up after you left. Those lists contain the names of every Amari in this city. If those people got their hands on the lists, the government could hunt us all down and," he pauses for a second, "—and kill us. No one would know. It would all be an 'accident.'"

"Then, why don't we just destroy the list?"

"We keep track of all of the Amari in the city and how the traits are passed down genetically. We are trying to find a pattern in the genetics when a normal person and an Amari have children."

"Are you on that list?"

He nods his head and looks up at me. "So are you."

My head is spinning. I have accepted myself as an Amari, but it is still shocking to hear my name on a list as important as that.

"I don't understand why we are such a threat." I can't think straight. My head is still throbbing, and pain engulfs my whole body.

"We have enhanced genetics, so we're stronger than the average person and are therefore considered a threat. Some people in the government cooperate with us, but most either completely ignore us or hunt us down."

I lay there in silence, wondering about who cooperates with us. Are they Amari? Will I ever be attacked like that again?

Luke stands up and places his hands on my cheeks. His thumb brushes the bruises on my cheekbones. "It will be all right. We are all in this together." He leans in and presses his forehead to mine. For a moment, I forget all of my pain, all of my worries, and all of my anxiety. All I focus on is him. His hands are on my face. Our bodies are inches from each other. Our heartbeats are in sync.

I look deep into his eyes, searching for anything. I find a young man who cares for me.

CHAPTER 13

TWO MORE WEEKS pass, and the last test for the first half of training looms near. For this test, we are required to fight Luke. As the leader of our training program, only he can accurately evaluate our overall improvement and progress. Luke will be the ultimate judge of where we will sit in the rankings and how many points we will have earned for this first section. Although I have fought him before, this time will be different. We've been on a date and kissed. How will that change the fight?

"Listen up! This will be your last test before your next month of training starts. This is weighed heavily against all of your other fights, tests, and training. If you win, you'll gain points and possibly move up in your ranks. If you lose but still improve from where you began, you will be given points but will most likely not move up in the ranks. Tomorrow, I will reveal the ranks and tell you how many points you need to make before the end of training in order to pass. If you are below the minimum, you better get ready to work hard next month because it is hard to get back above the line."

Luke looks at every student. I wonder if anyone is below the minimum. "Get ready to fight. We will go alphabetically according to first name. Alex Stone, you're up." I am not too worried about rankings or points. Paul and I are currently tied for first. One of us will have to beat Luke in order to remain in the first-place position. The other will drop to second.

I am the sixth person to fight Luke. Alex loses to Luke by one punch to the head, and Clara loses after a few good punches. Frank barely beats Luke. The other fights proceed in a blur. Only two people have beaten Luke so far.

I am called from my daze when Luke yells my name. "Kiara Smith. Ready to fight?"

"Yes. Are you? You look pretty beat up."

"That doesn't matter. Remember who I am and my strengths. Bruises don't affect me." Oh right. He is an Amari, and he is physically stronger than most Amari. His cuts and bruises probably don't hurt as much as they would hurt a normal person. My bruises must have been nasty, then, because they hurt for days. "I will not go easy on you."

Without a warning, Luke lunges at me and whirls his fist into my cheek. I stagger back, only to be kicked in the side. *Wow! He really is going hard on me.* With determination, I dodge his next punch and deliver a kick to his side.

"Giving up yet?" He tries to provoke me.

"You wish." I punch him in the chest three times in a row and kick him in the side. He responds with a punch to my face. Luke tries to kick me, but I grab his leg and try to flip him onto the ground. Instead, he pulls his leg back, carrying me along with it. I have to get up; I can't stay on the ground. I crawl away from him and hop up to my feet. Luke corners me at the edge of the ring and then tackles me. I thrust my knee into his chest, but nothing works.

Then, I remember back to our first fight. His soft spot is his stomach. I thrust my knee into his stomach. He flinches and releases me, so I scramble to my feet and face him. "Luke, no one's going to win, and we're just going to end up being beaten and bruised. Truce?"

Luke looks me dead in the eyes, and a grin spreads across his face. "Not now, not ever."

With a fire behind his eyes, he lunges at me and pins me to the ground again. He keeps his knees on my knees so I can't kick him. I try to wriggle free, but I can't. He holds me down, pinning all of my limbs. "Give up?"

"I don't want to, but I can't get out of this."

"There's only one option. I'll give you ten seconds like I do for every other fight." I scour my situation. There are no open areas or soft spots I can hit. Plus, my limbs are pinned. What is the only option? It hits me. His head is close enough so I can do it. I reach up and firmly press my mouth to his. Stunned, he loosens his grip on me. I whirl around and pin him the same way he pinned me.

"You must have forgotten about that option because you look really shocked."

"To be honest, I wasn't expecting it. But don't gloat now; you haven't won yet. In order for you to win, you have to punch me."

"Luke, I'm not punching you. We already went over this in our first fight. I'm not punching you in the face."

"I'm not going to try to wriggle free, so this is the only way for you to win. If you don't punch me, Paul moves up to first, and you're second."

I don't want that to happen. That can't happen. Having someone like Paul in first place would be a disaster.

"I care more about my life and about the ones I love than about my rank." I pause for a second. "But how can I pass up an opportunity to punch you?" I say, grinning. I punch Luke in the chest, hard enough for him to feel it and have to catch his breath, but not hard enough to leave a bruise. "I win."

Before he can say anything, I get up and walk out of the ring. I think I did the right thing; I did not completely hurt him, but I did not focus on my rank. In the next few fights, Paul loses to Luke. They exchange a few good punches, but Luke catches Paul off guard and pins him.

The next day, rankings come out. I am first with Paul in second. Alex, Clara, and Frank are all above ninth place, which means they are in a good spot for choosing jobs. Only two people are below the minimum: Maggie and another girl.

Paul glares at me from the opposite side of the room. Me being in first has made him furious. I can tell by the deadly look in his eyes.

Luke turns to us. "Well done, trainees. You made it through the first half of training. Go ahead and take Friday off, along with the weekend. We will pick back up on Monday."

As everyone leaves the classroom, Paul walks up to me. "I'm not going to let a girl like you stay ahead of me in the ranks. You better watch your back," he sneers. Then Paul walks away without another word. Being first means I will have a target on my back. I must be careful.

We all head back up to the dorms to say bye to each other. Like most of the trainees, I am going to spend the weekend at home with my family. We could go home and say our goodbyes on the first day of training, but they have not let us return home since.

"Where are y'all going for the weekend?" I ask.

"To my parents' house," Frank says as he packs clothes into an overnight bag.

"Same," Clara says.

"Yeah, I feel like it's been a year since I've seen them." A look of excitement fills Alex's eyes.

I finish packing my bag quickly and leave the dorm area. "See y'all on Monday!"

Before I can make my way downstairs, Luke catches my eyes and beckons me over. "Where are you going for the weekend?"

"To my parents' house. What about you?"

"I think I'll just stay here."

"But it's a long weekend. You should take a break from all of your work."

"Well, my parents are away on vacation, and I don't really want to go back to my house. So, I'm just going to stay here. Don't worry about me, though. Go enjoy your family."

I pause for a second, biting the inside of my cheek. "Why don't you come home with me? My parents would love to meet you, and I want to spend the weekend with you."

Luke scratches the back of his neck and thinks for a bit. "Okay, I'll come. Let me get some clothes first. Stay right there." He quickly walks back to his room. After ten minutes, Luke walks back towards me holding a duffle bag.

"Ready?" I look around to make sure no one is watching us, then I grab his hand and pull him close. I would feel anxious if I had to meet my girlfriend's parents, so I would try to reassure him the entire journey.

"What's your favorite part about being an instructor?" I want to take his mind away from my parents.

"Good." It's a tight little word.

"Good? Did you hear my question?"

Luke blankly nods his head. He's not listening to me; he is engrossed in his own thoughts. *What is he thinking about?*

"Luke." He glances at me, then focuses back on the road. "Are you nervous?"

"Yes." His knuckles turn white as he grips the steering wheel.

"Don't be. They'll love you."

Luke responds with a slight nod. I guess he really is nervous because he would have talked to me by now. Why is Luke so nervous? He is excellent with people, and my parents will love him.

We pull into my driveway and walk into my house. "Mom, I'm home," I yell into our house. My mom comes rushing towards me and wraps me in her arms.

"I missed you so much." She pulls away and places her hands on my shoulders, looking me up and down with pride in her eyes.

"I missed you too, Mom. Is Dad at work?"

"Yes. He will be home in a couple of hours. And Jacob is at his friend's house right now. He'll be home around 9:00." Her eyes then drift over to Luke. They hold each other's gaze for several seconds. Luke purses his lips attempting to release the tension.

"I don't think we have met. I'm Mrs. Smith, Kiara's mom." Luke stiffly shakes Mom's outstretched hand. *What was that all about?*

"Mom, this is Luke. He's the guy I have been hanging out with recently."

"Yes, ma'am. Kiara is excelling in training, and she is truly incredible to be around." He tries to smile, but his lips stay creased in a thin line.

"Well, I'm glad my daughter has found a respectable boyfriend." At the mention of the word "boyfriend," we both stiffen. Despite our history, we have never actually called each other that. We glance at each other, and I smile. His shoulders drop a little, and his tense posture becomes more casual.

"Anyway, your father and I have to meet up with a couple of people tonight around 6:00, so we will have to leave you two alone." She glances at us.

Luke steps forward and says, "Actually, Mrs. Smith, I was wondering if I could take Kiara somewhere tonight. It is very important, and I don't want her to miss it." Where does Luke want to take me?

"Very well. What time?" Despite her casual tone, it's clear she has expectations of him.

"Six o'clock." Her mouth presses into a thin line, and she turns to Luke.

"Where are you taking her?" My mom stares him down, waiting for an answer.

"Um," he is searching for the correct words, "it's a surprise."

"Very well." Her easy smile returns, and she walks into the living room. Why is my mom acting so strangely around him? "Come sit down. Tell me all about yourself." We walk into the living room and sit down on the couch. I sit next to Luke, and Mom sits in a chair facing us. We talk for a couple of hours before Dad walks into the room.

"Hello, Kiara." Jumping up from my seat, I run to give him a bear hug. I missed my dad so much. Returning my enthusiasm, he smiles into my hair and squeezes me. "I missed you too."

With a big grin on my face, I pull away from the hug. "Dad, this is Luke." I point to Luke, who has risen from the couch and now stands behind me.

"Hello, Mr. Smith." Luke shakes Dad's hand and then moves out of the way so he can sit down. I sit next to my dad, with Luke on the other side of me.

After a brief hour filled with laughter and light conversation, I wish my parents well as they head off to their meeting. We then walk to my car as Luke says, "I didn't want to say this in front of them, but I'm taking you to something Amari-related. It's sort of a meeting, and I want you to help me lead it."

"I'd be honored to help out, Luke." Nervous and excited, we get in the car and drive to the Amari facility. As we enter, I notice individuals gathered in small clusters throughout the room. Startled, I freeze in the doorway. How do they know about this place? Noticing my alarmed expression, Luke waves at them and leads me to one side of the room.

"Luke, who are those people?"

"Oh, I totally forgot to explain this to you. Those people are our fellow Amari. Since I am the head of all the trainers, it is my responsibility to find all the Amari in the Vigor group."

"How did you do that? It's not like you can just go up to someone and say, 'Hi! I'm Luke. Are you an Amari?'" I try to imitate Luke's voice to the best of my ability.

"First of all, I don't sound like that." He smiles at me. "Second, I haven't told you yet, but every Amari has two upwards-facing arrows on their hip bone." Luke lifts his shirt and pulls his waistband down a couple of inches. A thrill runs through me. Sure enough, there are two upward-facing arrows. It appears to be a triangle within another triangle, without the lines at the bottom. He puts his shirt and waistband back. "It can be hidden easily with makeup or clothing, but it is there, nonetheless. Lora helps me find all the new Amari among the trainees in the Vigor section. Someone else finds them in Intelligence and brings them here. Once you find an effective way to expose that area of skin, it is really easy to find all the Amari."

I always thought it was just a birthmark, but it turns out every Amari has this sign. Wait, how do they expose the mark? Did Luke use the method on me? Or did he just know that I am an Amari from my testing?

"Here's the point. We call this meeting every year to explain the whole thing to the new Amari, and I want you to help me explain it."

"I—I would love to help you, Luke. You have to tell me how you discovered the mark, though." He replies with a sly smile.

Out of nowhere, someone taps my shoulder. I quickly turn around and grab the hand. When I look at its owner, I blush. It's just Lora.

"Sorry. I'm a little on edge, and you scared me."

"You're fine. I'm Lora. We haven't really met face-to-face yet, besides that one time after Griffin beat you up."

I laugh. "I remember you, Lora. I'm Kiara, by the way." I shake her outstretched hand.

"I know. You're one of the only girls that can beat up Luke. Makes sense, though. You're an Amari, which makes you tough, and you're Luke's weakness because he likes you." My face turns red instantly. I glance back at Luke, who looks equally red. "Sorry. Did I overstep? I'm stronger with intellectual things, so I'm always analyzing and calculating."

"Why did you go into Vigor?"

"I wanted to be with Luke. We're practically family. Plus, I can pull off a Brawn job as long as I work hard. Anyway, did Luke ask you to help explain what an Amari is to the newbies?"

"Yes, I—" I am interrupted as the doors open. A man I don't know enters, followed by seventeen wide-eyed students. They are either from the physical training center or the intellectual training center. I recognize a few faces from the physical group. There is Sarah, a girl in the sports section, and ... Paul? I guess the people I don't like will have to be closer to me than I want. I recognize someone else. Frank? *Frank is an Amari? Who knew?*

Luke grabs my shoulder and turns me toward him. "There are seventeen newbies, eighteen including you. At the back of the crowd are three older Amari. Kiara, I think you will know two of them." From the back of the crowd, two men and one woman walk up to us. I know two of them. They are my parents!

CHAPTER 14

"MOM? DAD? When did you two become Amari?"

"Well, sweetie, we've always been Amari. We have been a part of this Amari group since high school, and they recently elected us as two of the four leaders. We knew you and Jacob would find out eventually, but we could not tell you. You two must figure it out on your own," my mom explains.

"Did you know Luke was an Amari?"

They both look at Luke and then back at me. My dad answers the question with a nod. I can't believe this. I'm not different from my family. I'm normal, kind of. That's good enough for me.

Luke turns towards the new Amari. "Listen up! You have been called here for a reason. All of you have something in common. You are all Amari." Murmurs instantly arise as the group discusses what he just said. He waits a few seconds to let them process this news. "This means you have enhanced physical or mental abilities."

"What exactly is an Amari?" Sarah asks.

My mom answers the questions. She says, "The Amari are small groups of people that protect the world from threats. Since we are a group inside the United States, we are designated to protect the U.S. and its citizens. Most major cities have at least one group of Amari."

Luke's hand grazes the back of mine. I grab his hand and say, "Every Amari has a mark on their left hip bone. It is shaped like two arrows, one on top of the other." I lift up my shirt and pull my waistband down just as Luke did to show me. I point to the symbol on my hipbone. "This can be easily hidden with makeup or covered up by clothing, but ultimately, it is the telltale sign of an Amari."

"How do we know you aren't lying? What if you are just trying to trick us?" Paul says in a skeptical tone. Although I want to punch him in the face for being so rude, I have to give him grace. I was also skeptical when I found out about the Amari.

"You don't. You just have to trust us. If you don't, then compare yourselves with your friends. Are you smarter or stronger than they are? Are you smarter or stronger than you should be for your age? Or you can look at the physical evidence. Do you have the mark on your hip bone?" Luke's answer silences the crowd for a few minutes as they think about what he just said.

After a couple of minutes of silence, Luke lets go of my hand and walks over to a wooden table. On the table is a bucket full of different colored bracelets. "Each of you will get one of these bracelets. Wear it at all times. This is how you will be notified when the Amari are needed. If and when you are notified, come to this building quickly. It is imperative that you do not ignore the call. Now, come choose your bracelet."

Luke dumps the bracelets onto the table and spreads them out. All seventeen walk up to the table and take a bracelet. Most of the girls get a colorful one or a bracelet with braids or beads. Most of the boys take the black cords or leather bracelets.

Luke walks back and hands me a bracelet. Gray and black cords twist together, forming a tight little braid. He puts it on my left wrist and looks up at me. "It matches mine. I thought you might like it."

Standing up on my tiptoes, I whisper into his ear, "I love it." I kiss him on the cheek and drop back down to my feet. "So, what else do we have to explain to them?"

"Just to be careful. Nothing too important," he says, winking at me. Luke turns to the group, who all have new bracelets on their wrists. "Do you all have a bracelet? Yes? Good. Now, one more thing. In our beloved country, some people think the Amari are dangerous. Important political figures often try to kill us off. If anyone ever asks you if you are Amari, always deny it. If you confirm the fact that you are an Amari, they will either take you in for testing or kill you. Once they know the truth, there is no returning to your normal life. Does everybody understand?" Everyone murmurs in agreement or nods their head. "Good. If you have any questions, come to us. If not, feel free to head home or back to the training facilities."

Frank jogs up to me as the crowd disperses. "So, I guess this is all real."

"I believe it. It makes sense."

"How are you already a leader? You explained this to us newbies, but you are a newbie."

"I have the right connections." I look back at Luke, who is talking to Lora.

"Oh. Mr. Scary Instructor over there is your connection?"

Puzzled, I playfully punch Frank in the arm. "Luke's not scary."

"He is, too. Luke always acts so tough and mean, and he beats you up in the ring."

"I thought you won against him."

"Yeah, by a punch. He still hit me pretty hard, though." Frank rubs the back of his head, feeling a recent bruise.

"Well, I like him. Don't tell Clara or Alex, though. I haven't really told anyone."

"What? About you being Amari, or about you dating our instructor?"

"Both. Promise?"

"Yeah, whatever. I guess I can't tell anyone, either. I don't want to die, so this is my only option." A grin slides across his face.

I shrug. "You get used to it."

Frank looks over to Sarah, who is talking with two other girls. Her bright red lipstick compliments her golden complexion, making her dusky blue eyes pop. "I was thinking about asking Sarah out. What do you think?"

"Go ahead. She's nice." I give him a playful shove as he turns towards her.

Frank walks over to Sarah, kindly asking her friends to leave. He then looks at the ground and mumbles something. I feel second-hand embarrassment for him; this is so hard to watch. Sarah smiles and blushes as Frank's face turns a light shade of pink. She nods her head, and they walk out of the building hand-in-hand. My heart swells with content; I'm glad it worked out for Frank.

After about ten minutes, everyone leaves except for a few leaders. I stare at the bracelet that Luke carefully picked out for me. It has little strands of silver embedded in the gray cord. It's beautiful. When Luke finishes talking to one of the leaders, I grab his hand and drag him out of the building. We stand in front of each other with our hands connected, Luke giving me a bewildered expression. "Yes, Kiara?"

"Luke Johnson, I have officially decided that I love you."

Luke stares back at me, our eyes meeting. "Well, that's good because I've decided that I love you, too." His grin is wider than mine, and there is a twinkle in his eyes. He pulls my arms around him and places his hands behind my head. Luke presses his mouth firmly to mine. An air of peace washes over me. This is my definition of happiness: my arms wrapped around Luke's neck, his hands draped across my back, the feeling of calm found only with Luke.

After several minutes, we pull ourselves apart. "Thank you for the bracelet. It really means a lot."

Luke squeezes my hand and says, "I'm not one for accessories, but I thought you would like it." I gently laugh as we walk back to the car.

When we arrive at my house, my parents are already asleep in their room. We sneak up to my bedroom and gently close the door. I switch on the lights. "Here's my humble abode. What do you think?"

He grabs my waist and pulls me onto the bed. We are sitting next to each other. "I think it's perfect." Looking around, he then adds, "So, where should I sleep?"

Oh, I didn't think about that. Blushing, I look over at him. This won't be weird. It's Luke. "I didn't think about it before, but the only option is my bed."

Luke tenses up a bit but forces himself to relax. He looks over at me. "Are you comfortable with that? I can sleep on the floor if you want."

"It's okay. You can sleep next to me." Without another word, I go into the bathroom to change into pajamas. Nervous energy courses inside me.

Luke is still sitting in the same spot when I walk out. "Luke, relax. You're okay." I place my hand on his shoulder. "Go get ready for bed. You don't need to sleep in those clothes." Luke solemnly gets up and heads to the bathroom, carrying a spare shirt and a pair of shorts.

Luke is always so gentle and careful not to overstep any personal boundaries. That's what I like about him. Most boys would jump at the idea of sleeping next to a girl. That's not Luke. He just sits quietly and makes sure I am comfortable. He never does anything unless I am comfortable with it.

When he returns, I flick off the light switch. The room goes dark as we carefully guide our way to my bed and hop in. Luke lays at the very edge of the bed, taking up as little space as possible. I find his hand and guide it to my shoulder, pulling him closer to me.

"Luke, it's okay," I whisper. I cradle my body beneath his and pull his arm around me. "Goodnight, Luke."

I hear a faint "Goodnight" and drift off to sleep.

CHAPTER 15

LUKE'S SOFT BREATH tickles my ear, pulling me from a deep sleep. "Good morning," he whispers. "How'd you sleep?"

I turn my body towards him. My face is inches from his. "Like a baby. How about you?"

"Well, let's just say I was too anxious to sleep."

"Luke, I told you not to worry. I want you here with me." Heat rises in his cheeks, so I change the subject. "Anyway, Mom probably made breakfast already. Do you want to go eat?"

Luke, filled with gratitude for the change in topic, exclaims, "Yes, I'm starving!"

"Good morning, you two. It's already 9:00. Were you planning on sleeping all day?" My dad is smiling as he takes a sip of coffee. He always makes fun of me for sleeping past 9:00 am.

"Good morning, Dad. I'm glad you got your beauty sleep, too. Where's Mom?"

"She went to the store to get a few things, but she should be back any minute. I think she left cinnamon rolls in the oven."

"Good morning, Mr. Smith." Luke changed into regular clothes—something about being put together in front of my parents. It's very sweet of him.

"Good morning, Luke. Sleep well?"

"Umm, yes sir." He glances my way, but I just smile back at him.

I sit down next to my dad, grabbing an iced cinnamon roll. My mom then walks through the door, holding a few bags. Without hesitation, Luke quickly grabs some of the bags and places them on the counter. In return, she gives him a smile of appreciation. Turning to me, my mom says, "I thought you would like cinnamon rolls. Afterall, they are your favorite." She gives me a big kiss on the head before unpacking the bags.

"Mom, you've really nailed the recipe," I say with enthusiasm while savoring the cinnamon roll. "But about last night. When were you both planning on telling me that you were Amari?"

My mom just shakes her head and smiles. "Well, we wanted you to find out on your own. We asked Luke to tell you your results for the Evaluation so you would have some guidance." I glance at him, and he grins. "After that, it was up to us to decide when we would schedule the next Amari meeting."

"Luke, you only instructed my tests because my parents asked you to?" Something deflates inside of me. I thought he was my instructor for most of my tests because he liked me.

"That was not the only reason. I would have done it whether your parents asked me to or not." Relieved, a grin spreads across my face.

"Now, stop talking to us. Go have some fun. It's not every day that you get the weekend off." My mom waves us out of the front door.

The weekend passes in a blur. Luke and I spend a lot of time together, just the two of us. Spending time with Jacob and my parents filled my heart with joy. I did not realize how much I missed them until I spent the weekend with them. Besides, my family really loved seeing this other side of Luke, the kind and loving boyfriend that I know him to be.

"Welcome back, trainees. I hope you liked the time off. Our main objective for the next three weeks is to explore effective training techniques. At the end of the month, you will have a final test and closing dinner."

This training is more manageable. We spend a lot of time in the classroom, learning about the best ways to instruct younger kids or older adults and all of the possible jobs we could have. The tests during the Selection, including the personality test, interest me greatly. It's fascinating how the personality test adjusts to individual experiences. So, that is what I want to be: an instructor for the Evaluation testing.

"That's it for today. I need to speak with Lora about something, so you can go now. Feel free to leave whenever you like. I'll see you in the classroom tomorrow morning." Luke leaves the classroom quickly. Whatever Luke has to clear with Lora must be important.

Everyone slowly files out, but I decide to wait in the classroom for Luke to return. Paul notices that I am lingering in the classroom and decides not to leave either. He waits until everyone is out of the room before approaching me.

"You're still ahead of me in ranks. You know what I think about that? I think it's pathetic," he spits at me.

Setting my jaw, I look him dead in the eyes. I must stand up to him and show no fear. "You know what I think, Paul? I think you're pathetic for thinking that. I earned my ranking. You earned yours."

"Was that an insult I heard? Never thought you were capable of that."

"I'm glad to be of service. Now, can you move? I have better things to do than make small talk with a second-place loser." My voice is like ice, smooth and sharp. It doesn't sound like me.

A movement catches my eye. I glance at his sleeve. Paul is pulling out a knife. Before I know what to do, he whips it out and presses the knife to my neck. "My dad told me two things growing up: I should fight for what I want, and men should always come out on top. I agree with him. No one would give a girl like you a second glance if you weren't first. I'm here to fix that. I want to be first, and I am ready to fight for it."

My arms are straining against his arm. The blade touches my skin. "Paul, what are you doing? The ranks mean nothing." My voice is strained.

"They do to me. My parents were both ranked first. I want the government job. The only logical thing to do is to eliminate any obstacles I have, including you."

"Are you insane?" My breaths are shallow as I strain against the knife. "If your mom was first, that means a woman came first in rankings and was offered the government job." I am grasping at anything I can find. Why does he care this much?

"My mom deserved her ranking. You don't." His voice is a sneer. I can barely breathe.

"We're both Amari. We're both supposed to protect each other," I rasp.

"I don't care about the Amari. It's just a stupid organization trying to take your money." The blade pushes deeper into my skin. Any further and blood will spill from the cut.

"Paul, I'll give you one more chance. Put the knife away."

He considers it for a brief moment but still pushes the knife into my skin. Blood trickles down my neck. That's it. I'm done with him.

I pull my knee into his groin. Paul drops the knife and holds his crotch. Adrenaline racing through my veins, I punch him three times in the face and kick him in the side. "I gave you a chance. I earned my ranking, and you can't take that away from me." Without another look at him, I walk out of the room, head held high. However, a twinge of pity plagues my conscience. Paul is only doing this because of his parents. They don't respect him, so he feels like he has to prove himself. I am glad my parents love me for who I am.

Luke is in the dorm hallway when I walk out of the elevator. He sees the blood on my neck and the cut from Paul's knife.

"What happened?"

"Paul tried to be intimidating, but I took care of him."

A sly smile slides across his face. "He won't mess with you again, I suppose."

"At least not anytime soon."

"Good." His eyes drop to my neck. Blood is slowly dripping from the cut. "Let's get you cleaned up."

Luke leads me to an empty room and offers me a seat on a couch. "I'll be right back." He leaves the room and returns minutes later with damp paper towels. There is a band-aid in his hand, along with some anti-bacterial wipes.

"First, we need to clean the wound." It's funny seeing Luke act like a doctor. I would never have thought of him as someone in the medical field. Humming a song I don't recognize, he brushes the damp paper towels over my neck, wiping the excess blood away.

"Next, we have to disinfect the wound. It might sting a bit, but trust me, you don't want tetanus." Luke places a wipe on the cut. It stings, but I grit my teeth and don't let a sound leave my mouth. My eyes start to water. "It's okay. You don't have to act tough here. It's just me."

I let a groan escape my lips before he removes the wipes. "Finally, cover the wound up with nothing better than—drum roll please—a band-aid." I laugh as he places the band-aid over the cut.

"You could be a doctor, Luke."

He replies with a slight chuckle. "That ship has sailed. Being a doctor means encountering everyone's pain and bearing it upon your shoulders. I could never do that."

"Well, if you ever reconsider, know that you have my recommendation." He smiles and leads me back to my dorm room.

"Try not to get into any more fights, Ms. Smith, or I might have to report you to the leaders."

"I'll try not to. Have a good night, Luke."

"You too." He winks at me before walking back towards the elevators. I then hop into bed and quickly fall into a dreamless sleep.

The rest of the section flies by. Paul avoids me at all costs, which is better than him watching my every move. For the last two weeks, all the trainees primarily stay separated, studying for the upcoming test that will determine our final rankings.

"Today is your final test. You will each take a turn with one of our instructors, who will quiz you on any material we have covered in these few short months. After, you will meet up with all the other trainees in the dorm rooms, waiting to be called for dinner. At 6:00 pm, we will have a closing dinner, and the trainees who passed the minimum score, along with the rank in each section of Vigor, will be announced. You will not be ranked with those in other divisions, such as those who chose sports or private security, but you will instead be ranked against those in the teaching section. Good luck to you all." Luke waves us off as we head to our final test.

This last test is the culmination of years of education, training, and testing. This test will determine what the rest of our lives will look like. I'm not too worried. I've been ranked #1 for the past month, so I am confident I will pass and move on to become a member of Strength. My biggest concern is whether or not I stay on top. If I drop in the rankings, I may not get the job I want— something that genuinely scares me.

Drawn from my thoughts, I look at the whiteboard. Next to my name, under "Instructor," is the name Luke Johnson. Of course. I smile to myself as I quietly walk to Luke's classroom, going over last-minute notes I took during training. When I reach his room, I take a deep breath before opening the door. "So, I'm assuming this is not a coincidence. You want to administer my final test."

Luke looks up at me and smiles. "Let's just say it's a coincidence. It sounds better when I have to explain it to the leaders."

"You know, you're the only one who has ever supervised my tests. During the Evaluation testing, you were always my instructor, and you are my instructor for the training section."

"Is that a bad thing?"

"I'd rather it be you than some stranger." Luke's grin makes me smile as I grab his hand, entwining my fingers with his. "So, what are we going to do today, Mr. Johnson?"

"Well, I am going to give you scenarios that might happen, and you have to answer or explain them. There's a right way to answer each question, and that's what we are looking for. Are you ready?"

Nodding my head, I sit down across from him and fold my hands in my lap. I concentrate on all the studying I have done and mentally prepare myself for the upcoming questions.

"How do you teach someone to perform a sleeper hold?"

"I would show them on a dummy and make them study the positioning of every part of my body. Then, I would let him or her demonstrate it on me before moving on to the next step. Finally, I would give them scenarios in which the student could perform a sleeper hold on their opponent."

"Good. Explain to me how the personality test works."

"The student is given a virtual reality headset. This headset portrays the scenarios that happen inside their head as images. Before the test begins, the instructor covers their mouth with a cloth soaked with an ointment. This makes the student feel as if the scenarios are real by putting them in a dream-like state."

"Name three ways to teach a student."

I take a second to recall all three ways. "First, I would explain each step of the move for the auditory learners. Then, I would demonstrate it for the visual learners. They can study my body's placement and mimic it. For the kinesthetic learners, I would have them practice the move on me."

Luke continues to ask me many questions about how to teach someone certain moves and other questions one would only know if they took his class. I answer each question to the best of my ability.

"That's all. Head back up to the dorms. I'll see you later tonight." Luke writes something on a clipboard, then looks up and smiles at me. All I can hope is that my results are good.

I get up from the chair and leave the room. When I reach the dorms, Clara greets me with a worried expression. Some of the other trainees from different sections wait in the room with us.

"How'd you think you did?" she asks me.

"Let's just hope for the best."

"You're going to pass, though."

"It's not the minimum I'm worried about. It's the rankings. This test could change everything."

"That's why I'm worried. I'm barely in ninth place right now. If my score on this test isn't good, then I might end up with an awful job."

I grab her hand and squeeze it. "Clara, you'll be fine. We're both going to make it. No matter what happens, whatever rank we get, we will always have each other."

Clara gives me a faint smile. "I sure hope so." Her eyebrows crease, and her lips press into a thin line. I have never seen her this worried.

Honestly, I'm not too worried. I'm confident that I passed training, and I firmly believe Clara did as well. For those who didn't pass, they are given little opportunity in life. They receive the jobs that no one else wants, and only a few of them get a chance at redemption.

A few years ago, a man was allowed to retake his testing with the next group a year later. He passed and became a successful lawyer. Unlike a majority of those who fail, he was given a second chance in life. However, this does not happen often, so everyone fears the possibility of failing the tests and becoming a nobody.

CHAPTER 16

A FEW MORE anxious students pile into the dorm rooms as we wait for the final dinner. Most people sit in silence, fiddling with loose strands of hair or vacantly staring at the wall.

After about half an hour, Lora walks in with a manufactured smile on her face. While she isn't the one receiving her results, she senses the anxiety in the room. Lora cares for each one of us and doesn't want to see us fail. "Time to eat!" Everyone is lost in their thoughts as she silently guides us down the stairway to the first floor.

Where the punching bags used to stand are silver tables full of food. Thirty tables seating four people each are spread across the room, twenty-five for the trainees and five for the trainers. The fighting rings are the only things left in their original place.

Matthew Carmen, the man who first welcomed us when we arrived at the training facility, stands in one of the four rings.

"Welcome, trainees, to the closing dinner. Take a seat wherever you please. We will eat dinner and then announce the rankings." Each student proceeds to take a seat at a table. Clara, Frank, Alex, and I sit at a table near the ring where Matthew stands. As soon as everyone is seated, fifteen waiters dressed in black and white come out and collect food from the silver tables. "Our waiters will serve you food. Feel free to ask for anything. Enjoy the meal!"

The meal is delicious: sirloin steak with a side of mashed potatoes and steamed vegetables. The food melts in my mouth. The room is quiet as everyone enjoys the meal, taking in each bite of food. However, the tension is evident as everyone awaits the results.

The time comes soon enough. The servers clear our plates from the tables, and then they leave the room without a word. We all look expectantly at Matthew, who now stands in one of the other fighting rings.

"Congratulations, all of you, for training hard for the last two months. The reward is great. I know all of you want to get to the rankings, but let's take a second to thank our trainers." A round of applause erupts. Matthew holds his hand up after a few seconds, and the applause slowly dies down.

"Now, to the rankings. I will first announce all who passed the standard and will be moving on as members of Strength. I will then go through each section, announcing the rankings of each trainee. To begin, I am very pleased to announce that, for the first time in several years, everyone has passed the standard and will be moving on to their new jobs." The crowd bursts into applause. I can't help but cheer with everyone. We are officially in Vigor. We made it. Our training paid off. Smiling from ear to ear, Clara gives me a big hug. All around us, trainees are hugging and kissing, depending on their relationships.

"Kiara, we made it!" Clara lets go of me and gives Alex a big kiss. What? *Did Clara just kiss Alex?* Frank rushes from the table and wraps Sarah in his arms.

Someone taps my shoulder. I turn around and see Luke standing there with a big smile on his face. "Congratulations! I had no doubt you would make it."

I don't even answer him. I grab his face and press my mouth against his. We stand there, pressed against each other. After a few seconds, I let go and wrap my arms around him. Matthew eventually taps the microphone, indicating that we should quiet down. Luke pulls up a chair and sits next to me, his arm wrapped around my shoulder. Clara kicks my foot under the table and gives me a shocked look. I haven't told her about Luke because I didn't want her to think he was biased. Now, I don't care who knows we're dating.

"We are all very proud of you. It has been at least a decade since every trainee in Vigor has passed. Our society will be very lucky to receive such fine, hard-working individuals." Pausing for a second, Matthew unfolds a piece of paper. It contains long lists of names and numbers. "For the rankings, I will move through each section alphabetically. Try to contain your cheers until the very end. First, architects and builders...."

Matthew continues through each section, including builders, farmers, police and protection, repair, recreational, sports, and many more. Finally, he reaches the training section. "Last, but certainly not least, the training section:

#1 Kiara Smith,

#2 Paul North,

#3 Frank Ceagan,

#4 Clarisse Taylor,

#5 Alex Stone,

#6 Daniel Sloan,

#7 Clara Larson,

#8 Margaret Goode ..."

That's all I need to know. My friends are all beaming with joy, and we can't help but let a few whoops and cheers escape our mouths. When he finishes the list, Matthew says, "Again, congratulations to all of you. Tomorrow, we will meet as a group for the last time. You will be choosing your jobs in order of ranking. I offer all of our first-place trainees positions in government. However, you can choose anything in your section. Get some sleep, and we will meet tomorrow."

We all rush up to the dorms, shouting and screaming in joy. I passed training; I am officially in Strength. Luke leads me to his dorm room and gently shuts the door behind us. Beaming, he grabs my hand and pulls me over to his bed. We both sit down, our legs hanging over the edge.

"How does it feel to be an official member of Strength?"

"It feels good." A sigh of content escapes my mouth. I made it. "It's all moving so fast. I haven't even thought about where I'll live or what job I'm going to get. What job do you have?"

Luke grabs my hand and rubs the back of it with his thumb. "I help instruct the Evaluation tests and a section or two of the physical training, but during the school year, I stay here and train people in workouts and fitness. And you can stay with me if you want. My house is a few minutes away from here, and that's where I live during the school year."

My heart begins to race. Live with a guy? I've never even slept in the same room with a guy besides those few nights with Luke.

He senses my uneasiness and says, "You don't have to if you don't want to, but I have an extra bedroom if you want it." Luke lets go of my hand and drops his gaze to the floor.

After a few moments of silence, I say, "Luke, I would love to."

He smiles with relief. "Anyway, I think I'm going to try out for a government job. I still want to train the new trainees and administer the Evaluation tests, though. Do you think I could do both?"

"Maybe. Just be careful, okay? The government is always looking for more Amari. Having a government job makes you more susceptible to being caught."

"I'll be careful." Despite the solemn topic, I grin and look down at my shoes. I would never have thought I would be sitting with the instructor I thought looked cute after having passed a whole month of strength training. I have made it so far in training and my relationship with him.

"Hey, do you remember that time I beat you in our fight?"

"Which one?"

"The first one, during our physical testing in the Evaluation."

"I let you win."

"No, you didn't. I beat you fair and square."

Luke laughs and tackles me onto the bed. We lay next to each other, staring up at the ceiling. "You know, I'm glad I asked you out on a date. Imagine if I didn't."

"Well, we definitely wouldn't be here right now. I'm just glad I had the nerve to say 'Yes.' The moment I first saw you, I had a crush on you."

"To be honest, when we first fought, I thought you were pretty cute."

"So, you had a crush on me?" A grin spreads across my face.

"I wouldn't call it a crush. I—"

"Well, I would." I laugh under my breath. A moment passes before I say, "Luke, can I stay here tonight?"

"Yes, of course. I mean, if you're comfortable sleeping in the same bed."

I look at him dead in the eyes with mock seriousness. "I think I'll live."

We spend the rest of the night lying on his bed and talking. I lay next to him, his arm around my shoulders, my hand on his chest. "Luke," I whisper in his ear, "I love you. Goodnight."

"I love you, too, Kiara," he whispers back to me. We fall asleep side-by-side.

CH/\PTER 17

I FEEL A TAP on my shoulder. "Time to go," Luke whispers in my ear. He is already fully dressed and tying his shoelaces. "I'm going to head downstairs and give you some privacy. The meeting starts in thirty minutes. Be there on time otherwise you won't get to pick a job. See you down there?"

"Yeah." I get out of bed and rub the sleep from my eyes. Today, I will choose to take a government job along with training the new Strength trainees.

Once I am ready, I jog downstairs and meet the rest of the trainees from my section. I pull Clara away from Alex and Frank so I can catch up with her.

"Hey!"

Before I can say another word, Clara grabs my shoulders and stares me dead in the eyes. "Kiara, you never told me you were dating Luke."

I just shrug and smile. "Well, you never told me you were dating Alex."

"We're even then, but you have to tell me about it later."

"Only if you do." We both smile and rejoin Alex and Frank. "Have you thought about what you are going to choose?" I ask.

"I want to be a workout trainer," Frank says. I imagine him talking to his trainees and planning the best workout schedule for them. It suits him. He has always been good with people.

"In high school, I had great mentors and teachers in my P.E. class. So, I want to be a P.E. teacher in order to help mentor other students." That fits Alex; he will be a great coach for high schoolers.

"Listen up," Matthew Carmen says. He sits behind a table that holds a stack of papers. "If you are in the training section, line up in order of rankings." Leaving my friends, I walk up to the front of the line. "Kiara Smith, congrats on getting first place. What job would you like?"

"I would like to apply for a government job, but still train and test the new twelfth graders."

"Wise choice. I can make that happen. Looking up at me, Matthew's smile is almost greedy. He waves me off and turns to Paul, who is next up in line.

Luke runs up to me as I leave the line; his eyebrows are creased. "There's something I need to show you." He grabs my wrist and pulls me up the stairs. We enter an empty classroom, where he shows me a video on his phone. I look to see what he is concerned about.

In the video, a group of masked terrorists holds the U.S. vice president at gunpoint. One of the men steps up closer to the camera and says, "We demand the president. Give him to us by the end of the month, or our little friend here dies..." he motions to the vice president, "... along with many more civilians." The video clicks off.

I look up at Luke. "What does this mean?"

"It means the U.S. might be entering a war soon." He looks vacantly out into space. "Or the Amari will be called in to protect the presidency. Unlike many local and state governments, the president and his close personnel respect us. They will often call us into service for things like this. Our city is normally one of the first to be notified because we are so close to Washington D.C."

"Are there any more Amari groups in the city?"

"No, but there are other groups in the surrounding cities."

Suddenly, I feel a buzz on my wrist. I look down at the bracelet Luke gave me. It is vibrating. Luke's bracelet is vibrating too. His eyes meet mine. "Let's go."

We jog down the stairs, skipping two at a time. Most of the people have left the main room by now. I see a few people on the streets. Some of them are heading to the Amari training facility.

When we arrive, most of the Amari are already there. Instead of seeing a large group of high schoolers and young adults, I see many men and women over the age of thirty. I had no idea there were this many Amari in our community.

"Welcome. All of you have been called here today because our president and our country are in danger. Terrorists have entered the country and are holding the vice president at ransom. His name is William Jones. They have called us to prevent any unnecessary publicity and threats. They are keeping this on the down low as of right now."

After a brief pause, the man continues. "This group must be near our city. We are five miles away from Washington, D.C., and William was last seen three miles away from the White House. Our job is to locate each member of this terrorist group and arrest them. Any questions so far?"

The man speaking, Greg Davenport, looks to be around 40 years old. He has black hair with gray flecks in it, and his glasses reflect the light from the ceiling. While he is not a 'veteran' compared to others in the room, he carries himself with a keen sense of leadership. I understand why the Amari designated him for this role. "So, we know the group is in the state. They call themselves the 'Grienzi.' They originate from Europe, but there is a bounty on their head because of the crimes they have committed in multiple different countries. Now, they are trying to take over the U.S. to get revenge on their home country, Spain. They have started by capturing the vice president."

I glance at Luke, whose crinkly eyebrows tell me all I need to know. The president is being threatened, and we have to fight terrorists. It's funny how your life can change in a matter of seconds.

"They have been known to wear black masks with a white stripe down the middle. It covers half of their faces, from the nose down." Greg pulls up a picture of the Grienzi on the screen. A group of gruff-looking men and women stand in a circle holding knives and other weapons. One man stands at the front, holding an innocent-looking man, the vice president, at gunpoint.

As Greg said, they all wear black masks covering half of their faces. The white stripe stands out, giving them some sort of unity. "We will split up into two groups. Those of us who are physically stronger and those of us who are mentally stronger. The mentally stronger will look everywhere for any info we can get on them. Look on the internet, social media, and anything that mentions the Grienzi. The president has given us special permission to access government documents in order to help the search. The physically stronger will train hard and be our scouts. They will eventually fight and take out the Grienzi when necessary. When we get any more updates from the president, we will alert you. You are dismissed."

As soon as the crowd disperses, I search for my parents. They are Amari, so they must be here. After a few minutes of searching, I spot them near the edge of the room and run up to them. I bury my face in my dad's shoulder. "Dad, Mom, I have to fight these people."

"I know, honey. It's scary, but you will have the rest of the Amari with you," Mom says. She encourages me as best she can while trying to hide her own fear for me.

"Where is Jacob?" A deep fear rises for my brother. Where is he? Is he safe?

"Jacob's fine. He is staying at a friend's house tonight. As of right now, he doesn't know about the Amari or that he is one."

"So, Jacob's safe?"

"Yes, he is." My mom smiles at my concern for my brother.

"Good. Will you two be fighting?"

"We are both mentally stronger, so that means we will stay here and research. I'm sorry we can't be out there fighting next to you." Dad embraces me and whispers in my ear, "But remember, Kiara, we're always here for you." I feel better knowing they will be safe, but I also don't want to fight without them by my side.

After a moment, he pulls away. "Since you are just as smart as you are strong, you could stay here and help the mentally stronger," Mom adds, with a hint of hope in her voice.

"Mom, I know you want me to be safe. But I could never rest knowing that I'm choosing to stay here instead of helping those who are out there fighting."

"I knew you would say that." The pride in her soft smile makes my heart swell. "You should probably get back to Luke then. We'll see you soon. We love you." Mom kisses my forehead.

"I love y'all." I hug both of them again and walk back over to Luke.

"Are your parents okay?"

"Yeah. They won't be fighting, which makes me feel better, but this is my first fight, and I don't know what the group will expect of me or how well I'll end up fighting and ..." Luke's eyes drift to the ceiling, and he starts shaking his head. "What?"

"What makes you think we've done this before? This is my first fight, too. I don't even know if I have the courage to fight terrorists." Luke looks down at his shoes, and the corners of his lips curve down.

"You're the bravest person I know. I would think you, of all people, could do this. Plus, I just assumed that you had been on crazy missions like this before."

"Thank you, but there hasn't been a major threat in seven years when my best friend died. I was thirteen when it happened. I—" Luke scratches the back of his neck. "I need to tell you something. Want to head back to my apartment in the training facility?"

We silently walk back to the training facility, tension and anticipation hanging between us. I remember back to when he was hooked up to the lie detector. Luke told me about how his best friend was killed, and he tried to save him. He didn't go into much detail, though.

When we reach his apartment, Luke quietly closes the door and walks over to the bed. Sitting down, he clasps his hands together and drops his eyes to his shoes.

I sit down next to him and put my hand on his hands. Luke looks up at me and takes a deep breath. "When I was thirteen, my best friend was captured and held for ransom by a terrorist group that I would prefer to leave anonymous. The terrorists contacted the governor, but since my friend was recently registered as an Amari, they didn't give him a second glance."

He continues, "All the terrorists wanted was money, but the government valued their own greed over the life of a child. The Amari tried to save him, but they couldn't reach him. I was desperate, Kiara. I couldn't let him die, so I tried to save him myself. When I reached the terrorists' hideout, I was stabbed in the side and left to die. My friend was then killed a couple of hours later."

Luke pauses for a moment. "Eventually, I was rescued and given medical attention, but he didn't make it. If only I was stronger, if only the governor would have listened to them, he would still be alive today."

A film covers his eyes as he recalls his pain. "But no, he had to die. I entered a dark time in my life after that. Watching your best friend die while suffering from a life-threatening wound does things to a kid. Lora has been there for me since the beginning, but his loss still impacts me every day." His voice quakes with each word.

"Hey, look at me." His eyes lift to mine. They are glassy with tears. "We're in it together. I will not let them do anything to you, and I will be there for you no matter what. I will not let you get hurt, okay?"

Luke nods his head and wipes the tears from his eyes. Taking deep breaths, he walks over to the window and stares out at the scenery for a few minutes. Attempting to change the subject, he says "So, we have the rest of the summer before our jobs start. What do you want to do? You know, besides fighting terrorists."

"I was thinking I could move in with you, and we could spend the summer hanging out with our friends."

"Sounds good to me." His voice is still shaky, but there are no signs of tears in his eyes. "Want to start packing now?"

"Yeah. I'll head to my dorm room to get my stuff."

I walk across the hall to the training dorm rooms. Clara is already there, packing her things.

"So, you and Alex. When did that happen?" I start piling my clothes on my bed.

Clara looks up at me and smiles. "Well, we started hanging out alone more. I thought it was really sweet that he wanted to get to know me. Then, Alex started doing more affectionate things, like hugging me when we were leaving for the night or holding my hand when we were alone on long walks. One thing led to another, and he kissed me! After that, we started dating." She looks off into the distance for a couple of minutes before bringing herself back to reality. "What about you and Luke? I could tell you liked him, but I had no clue you two were dating."

"Like you said, Luke asked me out on a date, and we started hanging out more. Turns out, we have a lot more in common than I thought." I smile and think back to when we were on the hotel's rooftop. The city lights were beautiful. We kissed for the first time that night. "Anyway, where are you moving?"

"Alex and I are going to get a small house. It's close to here. We'll have separate rooms and everything, but that way we can be closer to each other. What about you?"

"I'm moving in with Luke." Pausing for a second, I fold a few of my shirts and put them in a pile. "Have you heard where Frank is moving?"

"I think he's moving back with his parents. He might try to get a condo with Sarah or something."

"That's good. They're a cute couple." Once I finish packing all of my clothes, I hug Clara goodbye. "See you soon, okay?"

"See you soon, Kiara."

I leave her in the dorm room and meet Luke in the hallway. We walk out together, hand-in-hand.

We arrive at his house a few minutes later. Shrubs line the driveway, sitting next to bright pink rose bushes. Bees fly around the bushes, filling the air with a faint humming noise. When we walk inside, Luke leads me to an unoccupied bedroom. I put my clothes on the bed and follow Luke to the living room. "Your house is nice. Is it close to your parents' house?"

"They live ten minutes away from here. Also, my parents are both Amari, but they are in Italy right now, away from all of this chaos."

"At least they get a break before coming back to terrorists and threats."

Luke chuckles and grabs my hips, pulling me into a hug. "I'm glad you're here with me."

"I'm glad I'm here, too." Luke holds me in his arms for a few minutes. Peace overwhelms me as we stand together in silence. Closing my eyes, I soak in our closeness. This moment is perfect. The buzz of our bracelets interrupts the stillness. The Amari. I don't want this to end, but we have to go.

"I guess we have to leave now." Frowning, I pull away from him. He grabs my hand and says, "Come on. It will be fun."

Luke and I drive to the Amari facility but park a few blocks away so our little training facility doesn't seem suspicious. We walk the rest of the way to the building.

"Sorry to call you again, but we have a lead on where the Grienzi will be striking." My mom and dad are standing behind the man who is speaking. I remember them saying something about being two of the four leaders. "They will be gathering tonight in the trash yard twenty minutes from here. We will send three groups of sixteen Amari to investigate the area. Your groups are listed on the screens."

The man points to the left side of the room. Multiple screens are set up with projectors in front of them. I scan the lists for my name and discover that I am in a group with Luke. A sigh of relief escapes me. Since I can't be with my parents, I'm glad I am with Luke. Frank is also in my group. It will be nice to have two friends with me. "We will be heading out in an hour, so prepare in any way you need."

I rush over to my parents. "Mom, Dad, I'm scared."

"You'll be fine." It sounds like she is trying to convince herself instead of me. "Just stay with your leader, okay? Don't do anything stupid and stay safe. Fight your hardest." Mom's face is etched with worry. If my daughter was about to fight terrorists, I would be worried, too.

"Honey, no matter what, know we love you," Dad says. Although it's not as noticeable, lines of worry also stretch across his face.

"I'm going to go get ready. I love you all so much." They wrap me in their arms and kiss my head. "I'll see you when we get back, okay?" They nod their heads in unison. I walk away before tears stream down my face.

Luke runs up to me, looks me in the eye, and says, "We're in this together. I won't let anything happen to you." He leans down and kisses me between my eyebrows. A shaky breath escapes me.

Fear creeps inside me as we prepare for the ambush. Although I am with all of these people, I feel alone. No one knows my fear or my worry. I, as a young Amari, will be fighting among veteran soldiers. What if I am not good enough? What if I fail them? Sensing my anxiety, Luke places his hand on my back.

"Calm down. We're all in this together." His sweet smile eases some of my worry. Luke will be there for me. I know he will.

It's time to go. I grab an AR-15, strap it to my back, and follow my group outside. Our group will be facing the Grienzi head-on. Like I said, it's scary.

We hop into two black Suburbans, eight people crammed into each car. The drive to the trash yard is only twenty minutes, but it feels like an eternity. I sit in the back row next to Luke and Frank. Luke clutches my hand, his knuckles turning white. Everyone in the car is silent as we prepare for what is to come.

CH/\PTER 18

WHEN THE CARS pull up to the trash yard, we quietly file out and slowly creep up to the entrance. The other two groups get in position to flank the Grienzi while we attack head-on. I crouch behind Luke and another man from my car. We hold our guns steady, ready to pull them up to our shoulders and shoot if necessary.

The first man signals us to move forward. My heart is beating in my ears, and my palms are sweaty. We silently creep into the trash yard, hiding behind trash bags and old car parts. Once we are all on the property, our group spreads out into a straight line across the yard. We start inching our way to the building, guns pointed at the doors. I am in between a woman around the age of 30 and Luke. I feel safe knowing Luke is next to me.

We reach the doors with no sign of life. The leader of our group gently pushes the door open and slides into the building, followed by all fifteen of us. A gunshot is fired. We all drop to the ground, but no more shots are fired. Everyone is safe. My heart is in my throat.

We stay on the ground for several minutes, waiting for any more gunshots. When we are given the all-clear, everyone slowly gets up. I hadn't been breathing for the last two minutes. Gasping for air, I follow our group as we continue edging our way into the building. Suddenly, someone from inside screams, "The Amari are here!" as shots start raining down on us. After a brief moment of panic, Luke and I sprint behind a big wooden crate. I peer around the side. There are about thirty Grienzi members here. There are around fifty Amari members. We outnumber them easily. A shot whizzes past my head, drawing me from my thoughts. I shoot blindly around the corner. Gunshots are fired all over the room.

"You okay?" Luke screams next to me.

"Yeah!" I yell back to him. I can barely hear him with the noise. The air smells like gunpowder and smoke. I can't breathe, and my ears are ringing. Trying to suppress my coughs, I point my gun around the corner and fire at a man in a Grienzi mask. I quickly hide behind the crate again, not looking to see if I hit my target.

I glance at Luke. His face is rigid, and he is concentrating on a man I can't see. Reloading my gun, I put my foot out to steady myself and aim again. I focus all of my attention on one of the Grienzi. Before I can squeeze the trigger, a shot is fired. My leg feels wet. I pull back from behind the crate and look down at my left thigh. Blood has already stained my pant leg. It's just a graze, but it stings. Pain creeps up my leg.

Someone yells, "Retreat!" I can't tell which side is retreating, but I am grateful for the absence of gunshots. I pull myself up, putting all of my weight on my right leg. Luke slings his gun on his back and looks at me. His eyes run down my body, scanning for wounds. I notice his eyebrows crease and his lips purse as he catches sight of the stain on my leg.

"Are you okay?"

"It's just a graze." Despite it being a graze, blood steadily flows from the wound. Noticing this, Luke tears his shirt into a strip and ties it around my thigh. I wince at the instant pressure. Luke then wraps his arm around me and grabs my gun. I lean on him as we walk out to the trash yard. Once we reach the car, he helps me in and sits next to me on the drive back to the facility. Everyone is silent.

An older gentleman informs us that no one is seriously wounded or hurt besides a few cuts and scrapes. Two members of the Grienzi died. I feel guilty for their death, even though I am sure I wasn't the one who killed them. Another member of the Grienzi was seriously wounded and unable to flee. The Amari took him into custody and brought him back to the training facility.

My leg throbs. I bury my face into Luke's shoulder as he places his arm around me. In an attempt to distract me from the pain, Luke rubs my arm and plays with my hair, giving me goosebumps. Despite the effort, my leg still aches from the wound.

We make it back to the Amari training facility quickly. They shove the captured Grienzi member, who was blindfolded on the way here, into the building and remove his blindfold. I hobble over to the medics with Luke's help, ignoring the commotion over our new captive. Only five of us were wounded during the attack. An older man holds his arm, a dark red stain spreading down his sleeve. Another woman is dragging her leg to the table. Our leader said these were only cuts and scrapes, but these wounds look serious.

A doctor rushes over to me and motions for me to sit on a metal table. He unwraps the shirt Luke tied around my thigh and pushes my pants up so he can clean the wound. "This might sting a little." The man dabs alcohol around the wound. I grit my teeth and squeeze Luke's hand to release the tension building up inside of me. Alcohol in an open wound always stings. After he cleans the bullet graze, the doctor assesses it.

"The cut is deeper than expected. You will need a few stitches."

"Sir, are you sure? Can't I just slap a Band-Aid on it or something?"

"I know it's not ideal, but this is the fastest way for it to heal. The sooner we close the wound, the better."

By this time, my parents have rushed over. They are anxiously looking at the doctor and waiting for the decision. Luke squeezes my hand, lines of worry etched across his face. "How many do I need?"

"Only three. The cut is not that long, but the bullet graze is deep. If it was a few millimeters shallower, then you could, as you said, just slap a band-aid on it."

Information is swimming in my head. All I can think to do is nod my head in agreement.

"Okay. Lay down on the table. I'll go get a pillow and some numbing shots." After a few moments, the doctor returns with a pillow, numbing shots, and surgical tools. Among the tools, I notice a string with a small, pointed metal tip. That must be the string they use for stitches. I close my eyes as he inserts the numbing shots. I feel a slight twinge, and the throbbing in my leg slowly fades.

When I open my eyes, I see Luke staring at my wound with wide eyes. Luke's face tightens as if he is the one receiving stitches. He squeezes my hand and winces as the needle punctures my skin. My mom and dad hold my other hand, standing over me like watchdogs. They look as worried as Luke, but they are better at hiding it. I close my eyes again as I feel the prick of what I think is the needle sewing my skin closed.

"Done." I open my eyes and push myself to a sitting position. To perform the operation, they cut my left pant leg just above my thigh. There is a thin line with three stitches holding it together.

"It would normally take about ten days to heal. Since you're an Amari, it might be closer to five days. Come back then so we can check up on you. I will take out the stitches if the cut has healed."

I tear my eyes away from the stitches, meeting him with a smile. "Thank you." The doctor nods and walks away.

Luke sits down next to me on the table, and I lean into him. "Luke," I say shakily, "you look more worried than I do. I'm fine. It will only be a few days. Less than a week." He just grunts in response.

"You're so brave," Mom whispers into my ear. She gently kisses my cheek. "Now, listen to the doctor. You have to rest for the next couple of days. You got it? No chasing terrorists or bungee jumping off bridges."

"I won't, Mom. Don't worry." With a smile, I conceal my agony and terror upon realizing I've been shot.

Dad recognizes my pain and hugs me. "We have to go discuss some things with the leaders. We'll be right back, okay?" I nod my head. "We love you." They walk back to the group of leaders clustered at the front of the room, leaving Luke and me alone.

"Now that they're gone, what's wrong?" I look at Luke expectantly. Without a response, he just shakes his head. "Luke, I know you're upset. You might as well tell me because if you don't, I'll hook you up to the lie detector test." My attempt at a joke fails. He blankly stares at the floor, so I grab his chin and force him to look me in the eye. "Luke, tell me."

After a few seconds, he begins to talk. "I promised you I would not let you get hurt, but look where we ended up. What will happen in the real thing if I can't even keep you safe in a small ambush? You might end up like my best friend, dead." Luke pulls his face from my hands and looks back down at the floor.

"It's not your fault. During the fight, I put my foot out to steady myself. I should have just leaned against the box when I was aiming. Plus, it's not like I'm going to die. It's only going to be a few days before it's healed." Grabbing one side of his cheek, I pull him closer to me. I press my lips to his ear and whisper, "Luke, you're still the most reliable person I know. I would put my life in your hands. This is not your fault. Okay?"

Luke turns his head to face me and looks me dead in the eyes. His posture sags and his eyebrows are raised with concern. I grab his hand and entwine our fingers. "Promise me you're okay, Kiara."

"As long as you promise that you will not worry about this. It is not your fault."

"I promise." His eyes fall back to the floor as he fades into deep thought. After a few minutes, he looks back up at me and smiles.

"Feeling any better yet?"

Luke grins. "Well, you do have a way with words. Want to leave? Our work is done for the day."

"Yes." After I wave goodbye to my parents and Frank, Luke and I leave. Luke offers himself as a crutch, taking most of the pressure off of my leg.

When we arrive at his house, I walk into his bedroom and sit on the bed. Luke follows closely behind me, his hand on my hip to steady me. I look down at my torn jeans, sad that I will not be able to wear them in the future. Noticing my expression, Luke walks over to his closet. "Do you need pants? I have sweatpants you can wear until you get more clothes."

"That'd be nice." Luke pulls out a pair of gray sweatpants. He turns around as I slide my pants off. Steadying myself on his bed frame, I grab the sweatpants and slowly slide them over my stitches.

"Done?"

"Yes. You can turn around now."

"I have to get a new shirt because mine is ripped from tying up your leg. I'll be quick, though." Luke turns around and rummages through his closet for a clean shirt. He pulls his ripped shirt off and throws it to the floor. After a few moments, Luke faces me as he pulls the clean shirt over his body. Before it falls into place, I catch sight of a scar on the left side of his body. I walk over to him and gently lift his shirt, revealing his scarred skin. I softly run my fingers over the scar, sensing his stiffness.

Luke's eyes drop to my fingers and flick back up to my eyes. He looks embarrassed by the imperfection marring his perfect skin.

"Is this the stab wound?"

"Yes." Luke pauses for a moment. "I don't let many people see it. Anyone, for that matter. This scar is a sign of weakness that I have to live with for the rest of my life. It's a constant reminder of my grief and my failure."

That hits me hard. Imagine having a mark of your failure for the rest of your life. It is a constant reminder of his best friend's death, how Luke was left to die, and his own hopelessness. But it's also a reminder of his perseverance and courage through the scariest situations. "I think it's a battle scar—something that makes you stronger than you were."

Luke grins at my new perspective and grabs my hands, diverting the attention away from himself. He sits on his bed and pulls me down next to him. "You know, for the next five days, you'll have to stay off your leg."

"Yeah, I know. Probably won't happen, though."

"It's going to have to happen." Luke laughs and lays back on the bed, his blue eyes searching the ceiling. I lay back next to him, placing my hands on his chest. "Do you ever imagine what life would be like if we weren't Amari?"

"It would be pretty much the same. I would be with you and my friends. I wouldn't have this wound, though, so that would be a plus."

Luke smiles. "No matter what we are, we would still end up together."

CHAPTER 19

I AWAKE TO LUKE'S heavy breathing. Luke and I must have drifted off to sleep when we were talking. When I check the clock. It's 2:00 AM.

My body is stiff from the past day of fighting, and my left leg aches from the stitches. I need to loosen my muscles; I need to walk around for a little bit.

Slowly getting up from the bed, I sneak out of the house. The cool air sends chills through my body. Crickets quietly chirp, breaking the nighttime silence. As I walk down the sidewalk, I take in my surroundings. Luke lives in a nice neighborhood surrounded by manicured lawns and neat shrubbery. Each house has the same structure. The only differences are the paint color and the rock on the house.

I limp over to the nearest bench and sit down. At night, the world is peaceful and quiet. It is the best time to walk, think, and explore. I let my mind wander over the last couple of days. I am no longer a trainee but a full member of Strength. Within the past two days, I have been called to the Amari facility twice. I participated in my first fight, and I shot a gun at someone for the first time. I have also been shot, received stitches, and moved in with a guy. Compared to the rest of my life, I have had a very eventful week. To top it all off, I am sitting on a bench at 2 o'clock in the morning in a strange, new neighborhood. Closing my eyes, I let the fresh air wash over my body. Nothing could make this week stranger.

Footsteps startle me from my peaceful state of mind. I quickly get up from the bench and crouch behind it. What is it? An animal? A person? A gang? I hide in the shadows as best as I can, hoping for safety from whatever is up this early.

Across the street, a man and a woman slowly approach each other. She is a tall blonde with a rigid posture. The man is a burly guy with dark, mousy brown hair. He sways when he walks, suggesting he drank one too many drinks. They are both wearing black masks that cover half of their face with a white stripe down the middle. The Grienzi! I sink further down under the bench and try to listen to their muffled voices.

"Those scum, the Amari, they found us," the male says. His voice is rough like sandpaper scratched his vocal cords.

"Any injuries?"

"A few scrapes. Nothing too serious except for two dead on our side in the midst of the brawl. They got another one of our men, but he shouldn't say anything. We gave the Amari some cuts and bruises. I heard one or two of them had to get some stitches." He chuckles under his mask as heat rises in my cheeks.

"That doesn't matter. We have to find a secure location."

"Where do you want to meet, boss?"

"The mall, second floor."

The man pauses for a second as if in deep thought. "No offense, but that's kind of obvious."

"Exactly. They won't expect us. Meet me in the emergency stairwell tonight at 9:00. I'll get the alarms turned off. Plus, no one uses that stairwell."

"Yo, boss, I don't think the entire crew can fit in there."

"Do you think I'm an idiot? Only bring four or five members. Leave the rest at the base. Okay? Do you think you can do that?" She speaks in a sarcastic tone, suggesting that he is just as stupid as his question.

"I'm not dumb. I can remember things. See you tonight with five members at the mall, on the second floor, in the emergency stairwell."

"Congrats. You're not stupid. See you then." She walks away without another word and, after ten yards, pulls her mask off. He walks down a different street and eventually pulls his mask off, too.

This is significant information. Just moments ago, I witnessed a Grienzi meeting, and I know where they will meet next. I need to tell Luke. With this mission in mind, I get up from behind the bench. Someone is standing right behind me. I scream, but his hand is already over my mouth. I try to kick him, but he wraps his leg around mine. I'm stuck—my stitches sting. I don't know what to do.

"Calm down, will you? It's just me." That voice sounds familiar. Luke. I gasp and stop struggling. It's just Luke. He lets go of me, and I turn toward him.

"How long were you standing there?"

"Only for a minute or two. When I woke up, you weren't there. I freaked out. You owe me one, you know."

"Let's head back to your house. I need to tell you something important."

We walk back to his house quickly. My wound stings, but I ignore the pain. When we reach the house, I close the door behind us and turn on the lights. "Luke, I just witnessed a Grienzi meeting."

Luke stands there for a second, speechless. "Are you sure you're not hallucinating? That can be a side effect of the painkillers."

"I'm serious. The boss, or leader, or whatever she is, met someone we fought with yesterday. They're meeting tonight at 9:00 in the stairwell on the second floor of the mall."

His body stiffens as he considers whether or not this is true. "Are you sure? If you are, I will report this to the leaders in the morning."

"I wouldn't joke about this. I'm sure."

"Okay. Since it's the middle of the night, everyone is probably asleep. Let's go back to bed, and I'll call this up bright and early. Sound good?"

Dizziness overcomes me as I nod my head. The adrenaline starts to wear off, and my body starts to sway. "Yes. Thanks, Luke."

Luke grabs my hand and leads me back to bed. I climb under the covers next to him, grateful to be lying down again. "How's your leg?"

"It's only throbbing."

He finds my hand under the covers and laces his fingers with mine. "We'll have to be more careful tomorrow so you can heal."

"Luke, promise me you won't go fight tomorrow. I need you, and I want to know you're safe."

He closes his eyes for a moment, thinking of a response that will satisfy me. "I can't promise anything, but I'll see what I can do. Now, get some rest. You need it."

"Okay." I close my eyes and let sleep drag me down into its depths. "Goodnight, Luke," I whisper.

"Goodnight, Kiara."

CH/APTER 20

"LET'S GO." Luke gently shakes my shoulder. Sleep still drags at me. I open my eyes and squint, slowly adjusting to the light. Luke is already fully dressed and ready to leave.

"Give me five minutes." Before I get out of bed, I check the clock. It reads 5:00 AM. Luke really meant early because the sun is not even up. I walk to the guest bedroom and dig through my clothes to find an outfit that matches. I look down at my wrapped leg. It doesn't hurt as bad as it did last night, but it is still throbbing. I throw on a pair of baggy jeans along with a white shirt. "Ready."

As we drive to the training facility, Luke calls the leader. I am too tired to fully understand what they are saying, but I hear Luke say keywords like "Grienzi" and "mall." As we drive, I focus on the scenery that we pass, trying to take my mind off of the Grienzi. After a few minutes, I spot the bench I sat on last night and the crosswalk where the late-night meeting took place. I can't believe that happened three hours ago.

After Luke ends the call, my wrist vibrates. Mr. Davenport must have alerted all the Amari, assuming that they get up at 5:30 every morning.

We quickly drive to the training facility and meet the rest of the Amari. When we walk in, they all turn to us. "This is Luke and Kiara. They are the ones who called this meeting. Give them your undivided attention," Greg Davenport says.

Luke looks down at me and whispers in my ear, "Just tell them what you told me."

I nod my head and look into the crowd. "At 2:00 this morning, I encountered the leader of the Grienzi. She was meeting one of the members we fought with a few days ago. She stated that they would be meeting tonight at 9:00 PM in the mall. The group will gather in the emergency stairwell on the second floor. Five members of the Grienzi will be present, along with the leader. The security systems will be down, so the alarms won't turn on when the doors open." Once I finish, everyone turns to a neighbor and starts whispering.

Greg draws the audience's attention back to himself. "Okay. As usual, the mentally strong will research the best way to attack." About half of the group splits off towards the computers and tables. "The rest of you will have to fight. We will use the same groups as last time to keep it easy. However, there will be a few changes. Group 2 will attack head-on, not Group 1. Also, the injured will not fight. You have the day to prepare. Please stay near this facility and meet us back here at 7:30 PM. Thank you." Greg walks off to a group of older men and women, which include my parents.

I turn to Luke. "Remember your promise? You're staying with me. I couldn't stand it if I stayed here while you were risking your life somewhere else."

"Kiara, I have to go. Greg needs me to help protect the group. Don't worry about me, though. I'll be back before you know it."

My lip quivers, but I force it to stop. Luke is leaving me. If he's not staying here, then I'm not staying here. I'm going on this mission. "I'm going too, then."

"No, you're not." Luke puts his hands on my shoulders. "You're injured. There is no way I am going to let you leave, and you can't tell me otherwise. Okay?" He sets his jaw and crosses his arms.

I observe the groups as they prepare and train. I can't let them go while I sit here helpless. I nod my head, but I can't bring my eyes to his. I'm going on this mission even if he says I can't.

Hours pass before it's time for us to leave. I wallow in my guilt, unable to look Luke in the eyes. I hate lying to him, but I can't sit here and let others do the dirty work. It's not who I am. I need to be with them, fighting.

All of the Amari suit up and ready themselves to leave at 8:00. Luke kisses my forehead and embraces me. "Don't leave. I'll be back before you know it." I try to smile at him as he walks out of the building.

Group 1 and Group 2 leave first; Group 3 waits by the door for their signal to leave. I will not stand here while people risk their lives. I am determined to go on this mission. Slipping into the middle of the group, I walk out with them and climb into one of the trucks. The drive to the mall is quick. I share the car with two women older than me and a boy I recognize from school. I think he is two years older than me.

When we reach the mall, we are told to spread out. The leaders give us a few disguises so that we can blend in with the other shoppers. Some men are given caps and cups of water. Some women are given sunglasses and even new outfits. A group of three girls are given dresses and heels to wear. Supposedly, they are on a "Girl's Night Out."

I am given a Chanel bag filled with wrapping paper, supposedly holding a bottle of perfume. We are then split into groups of two, except for the occasional group of three. When everyone is ready, we slowly make our way to the second-floor stairwell. Since we are in Group 3, we are instructed to wait on the second floor, watching the stairwell doors.

The boy named Peter Lynn, who was in my car, is my partner for this mission. We "shop" in the surrounding stores, waiting to be called into action. While we wait, he makes small talk about our date we supposedly had last week; we are posing as a couple. It feels weird acting like I am dating someone other than Luke. It's almost as if I am betraying him.

Once we are about twenty yards from the stairwell door, we stop and sit down on a bench. When I look around, I can pinpoint each of the Amari who are scattered throughout the mall. I wonder where Luke is.

Peter turns to me and starts a basic conversation. "So, Kiara, what did you buy?"

I stare at him blankly; I didn't buy anything. Noticing my confusion, his eyes flick to the bag that I am holding. I take his cue and say, "While you were in the bathroom, I got a perfume from Chanel. It's rose-scented."

"You must try that on later." Peter winks at me.

I feel sick to my stomach. Is he flirting with me? I shove my emotions to the side and let out a fake giggle. "You know I will."

"So, let's talk about lunch. How about we eat at that new—" Peter's voice slowly trails off as he looks past me. His face freezes, and his body tenses up. His mouth, which is barely open, whispers, "There's a man standing across the hall holding two pieces of paper. One of them is a list of ten names and faces, and the other is a sign that says '$1,000 for every Amari brought to us.' He's staring at us." His eyes then skirt to mine. Peter grabs my face in his hands and pulls my mouth towards his. We lock lips for what feels like an eternity before he pushes me back. He looks back past my face and sighs.

I am stunned. My face is slack, and I don't know what to say.

Peter catches on to my expression. "Sorry. Most people tend to look away from couples showing PDA. That man looked suspicious of us, so I thought that if we made him uncomfortable, he would look away and move on. I just didn't want to get caught." He looks down at his hands for a second, puts a serious face on, and resumes our undercover alias as a couple. "I had fun yesterday. We definitely need to go there again."

I am still shocked, but I need to carry on this persona. "Yes, it was so fun. I loved their steak."

"It looked so good. I thought the chicken tasted amazing."

"Do you want to go tomorrow night?"

"Sounds great."

Our wrists buzz, calling us back to the trucks. We will know what happened when we get back to the facility. Since we weren't called into action, I think the news is good.

On the drive back, Peter and I sit in silence. What can you say after kissing a stranger?

"About the kiss, I'm sorry I didn't warn you. It wasn't my right to assume you could just kiss a man."

"It's okay." How will I tell Luke?

Peter hesitates momentarily before asking, "Would you like to have dinner together?"

Heat rises to my cheeks. "I'm sorry, but I have a boyfriend."

He blushes from embarrassment. "Oh, sorry."

"No, it's okay. His name is Luke. He's your age, I think."

"Yeah, I know him. You're a lucky girl. Most of the girls in our grade fawned over Luke, but he rejected them all. You must be a really special girl if he accepted you."

"Actually, Luke asked me out on a date, not the other way around."

"He must really like you then." Peter gives me a genuine smile before looking out the window of the truck. Without looking at me again, he says, "I'm going to tell the leaders about that Amari list. Do you want to come?"

"Thanks for the offer, but I really need to talk to Luke. Can you do it alone?"

"Yeah, of course. Just thought I'd offer." The rest of the drive is filled with silence as we both process the last couple of hours.

When we reach the facility, I see the other groups gathered together in small clumps. That means Luke's group got back before us. I peek out of the window and see Luke standing at the door to the facility with his arms crossed. When he sees me hobble out of the vehicle, anger rises in his chest. He storms to the truck and stops a few feet in front of me. His arms are crossed, and his face is pinched.

I drag Luke to a neighboring building to talk to him alone. He does not yell at me or scold me, but just stands there in silence. That is way worse. I would much rather take the screaming up front than the building tension that is about to explode. I can tell there is a mix of anger, hurt, and fear in his face.

"Luke, I—" I can't look at him. Guilt weighs me down, beckoning me to run away from what's standing in front of me.

"No, let me go first. I come back from the mission and find that my girlfriend is missing. Her parents don't know where she is. Neither do the doctors or the leaders. I start to panic. What if she is hurt more than she already is? Or captured, even? And then, she gets out of a truck that went to the mission. The one thing I told you not to do in order to protect you from further harm, you did. How do you think that makes me feel?" Luke is furious. His face is red from screaming, and his arms are waving in the air.

My eyes drop to the floor, followed by my head. The guilt pulls me down. I feel like a puppy being chastised for something I did wrong.

He persists, "Kiara, remember you made a promise to me not to go. You broke a promise and lost all of my trust along with it." His eyes are filled with pain. His tone and the way he looks at me reveals his emotions: anger, pain, sorrow, and fear.

"I—I'm sorry. I had to go; I couldn't bear staying behind. Being in the third group meant there was no chance of us fighting. Plus, I was with a boy from your grade, Peter Lynn. Remember him? He would have protected me."

Luke stands as still as stone.

"I just couldn't sit on the sidelines while others went to fight. I feel even worse because—"

He sighs, releasing some of the tension from his body. "Kiara, I just need some space right now. Just give me a couple of hours to cool off, okay?" Luke turns around and walks out of the building without another word.

Tears well up in my eyes. I still need to apologize to him and tell him what happened with Peter. I slide to the ground and cup my face in my hands, needing Luke now more than ever.

CHΛPTER 21

HOURS PASS WITHOUT a single word. I lean against the wall of the abandoned building, regretting everything I have done in the last few hours. How could I be so stupid to go on a mission without Luke's knowledge? He cares about me. Luke was just trying to protect me and keep me safe, and I completely ignored him.

Where is Luke now? Did he already move on to another girl who will ease his worries and obey his wishes? Or is he crying in his room like I am now? My body aches for him, and the thought of living without Luke brings a fresh round of tears to my eyes. Surely, he will come back for me.

After another long hour of sorrowful tears, I hear a knock at the door. "Hello?" It is a soft, innocent voice that is muffled by the door. Who is it?

"Come in." My voice is hoarse from crying so much.

A tall man with dark blue eyes and brown hair walks in. It's Luke. "Hey. I thought you would still be here." He gives me a weak smile before sitting down beside me.

We sit there, side-by-side, for a few moments. The tension between us slowly builds with the silence. I have to apologize to him.

I wipe my eyes. "Luke, I'm so sorry. I should have listened to you. All you wanted to do was protect me, and I was so blinded by my selfish thoughts that I couldn't even see how much you loved me. Then, I went anyway without you knowing and made you worried and stressed. And when I was at the mall, I—"

"No, Kiara, I'm sorry. I snapped at you, and I shouldn't have. This last week has just been crazy with the Grienzi and you moving in with me. Plus, it's not my right to confine you in the building when you want to go elsewhere. You know your limits, and I have no right to constrain you. Please forgive me."

"I will always forgive you, but I don't deserve your forgiveness. I need to tell you—"

Luke pulls me toward him and presses his lips against mine. *I can't do this. I betrayed him; I can't.* Reluctantly, I push him away and stagger up. *I can't lie anymore.*

"Luke, just listen to me. I kissed another boy. I kissed Peter."

He just stares at me, not sure how to take the news.

"We were undercover during the mission as a couple," the tears are welling up in my eyes, "and this Amari hunter was staring us down," the tears run down my face and my voice shakes. I never knew I could get this emotional this fast. "And Peter just kissed me. I didn't know what to do. He said it would make the hunter look away because people tend to look away from kissing couples." My words are barely audible now.

"And then he asked me out, and I said 'no' because I have you. Or, I guess by now, I had you. You'll probably break up with me for real this time, and then I won't have the one person I love dearly and—" I am fully crying now. I can't talk. All I can do is stand there, wiping my eyes, as the tears stream down my face.

"Stop crying," he says. His voice is stern, but not harsh. Luke stands up and faces me. After a few minutes, I calm myself down. He gently grabs my face and rubs my cheekbones with his thumbs, drying the rest of my tears. "I forgive you."

"What? I don't deserve—" Luke presses his lips to mine. Instead of pulling back, I press further into the kiss. This feels right. I place my hands around his neck, and he moves his hands down to my waist. A shudder travels down my spine. Luke slides his hands under my shirt and rubs the small of my back.

"Let's just forget about it, okay?" I nod my head in agreement. "We should probably head back to my house," he whispers into our kiss.

Confused, I pull back as my hands drop to my sides. "What about the meeting?"

"Seeing as it's 1:00 in the morning, I think they are all in bed."

"But we just ended the mission? How is that possible?"

"Well, the mission ended at 10:00 PM. It's been three hours since we got into that fight. That's why you're so tired."

"Is it that obvious?" I say with a yawn.

"A little bit." Luke smiles and grabs my hand as I limp to the door. "Today, they interviewed the Grienzi guy who was captured during the first fight. They displayed it on the screen, but the audio was turned off so we couldn't hear anything. It was really boring to watch."

"Well, I'm glad I didn't have to watch it." Once we reach Luke's car, I unwrap my leg and look at the incision. It is scabbing over. In a day or two, it will probably be a scar.

Luke hops into the driver's seat. "You want to go for a late-night stroll?"

"Well, I can't walk for that long because of my leg, but we can find a place to sit if you want."

"That's good enough for me." Smiling, he drives through his neighborhood and parks near a bench. Luke opens my door and helps me out. We then slowly walk over to the bench and sit down next to each other.

"So, how was the kiss?"

I shove Luke's shoulder. "You said you would forget about it."

"I know, but it's a valid question. How was it?"

"Well," I hesitate for a second, "it was kind of weird. To be honest, I didn't even know what was happening until it was over." I glance up at Luke, who is listening intently. "Anyway, how was your group? I basically just walked around and acted like I was shopping."

"We were all clustered around the door of the first-floor stairwell. I was assigned to walk around with two other boys. One of them was Frank, and the other was a boy from my grade."

"I guess you didn't kiss any of them, did you?"

Luke laughs. "No, I didn't kiss them." I am glad he is smiling. "The Grienzi still escaped, though. I don't know how they pulled it off. We had them cornered in that stairwell." We sit in silence for a few seconds, thinking about how they evaded us.

After a few minutes, I grab his hand and lace our fingers together. My leg hurts a little, but I ignore the pain. "Luke, you're a great boyfriend."

"Yeah, well, I try my hardest." I grin and lean my head against his shoulder. "Now, let's get you to bed before I have to carry you there."

CHAPTER 22

"SO, WHAT HAVE you been doing lately? I feel like I never get to see you anymore." Clara invited me to go to the mall with her. Even though it has only been a week, it feels like I have not seen her in ages.

"I've just hung out with Luke. We moved in together, which has been a little chaotic."

"Really? That's so exciting!" Her genuine tone makes me smile.

"And I saw Frank the other day. I think he's still dating Sarah, but I didn't ask him about it. What about you?"

"Alex and I have been together a lot. I am just so lucky to have him." Clara looks off into the distance, then snaps back to reality. "Tell me again why you had to get stitches."

"I fell on a rock, and it cut my thigh open. It wasn't that bad, though, so I only had to get three stitches." I avert my eyes while

I talk. I hate lying to Clara. She is my best friend, and I don't want to keep secrets from her.

"That's weird. In your text, you made it sound like you were hiking and ran into a stick."

My pulse quickens. What do I say now? "Well, I was hiking." Think, Kiara. "I slipped on a wet rock, and I fell onto a sharp stick. It didn't really hurt, but I still had to go to the ER."

"Oh. I hope it doesn't hurt that bad anymore." After a brief pause, she says, "You must have cut it right after we completed training because it is practically healed."

That's something else I can't let Clara know about. Being Amari means I heal faster than a normal person. "Yes, I fell around that time. It's almost healed, so it doesn't hurt that bad. Hopefully, I will get the stitches out tomorrow."

"If you need a buddy, I'll come with you. I have nothing to do tomorrow." As she says this, she glances to the left and spots a store. Clara drags me into it before I can say anything. "We're going to do makeovers. You pick out something for me, and I'll do the same for you. It will be just like old times."

With a joyful smile on my face, I search the store for clothes that would suit Clara. I come back with a yellow sundress and a jean jacket. She gives me a short, light pink dress and a cute hat. We try on the clothes.

"You look so cute in that jacket." I wink at her.

Laughing, she says, "You don't look too bad yourself." Clara pulls her phone out to take a picture. We pose, and she takes a picture of our reflection in the mirror. We change back into our original clothes, and then she says, "Let's get another outfit!"

Before we search the store again, a short man walks towards us from the entrance of the store. His vaguely familiar face looks me up and down, sending shivers down my spine. "Having a nice time, ladies?" His harsh voice overpowers the quiet whispers in the store.

"Yes sir."

"Do I know you from somewhere, young lady?" He stares at me, setting my whole face on fire. He doesn't look away.

"Um, no." I look down at my feet. He keeps staring. I feel uncomfortable, so I grab Clara's arm and whisper into her ear, "We should go now."

"You aren't going anywhere." He grabs Clara's arm and yanks her back towards him. Then, he pulls out a gun and points it at her head. "Where are the Amari? Tell me and you can have your stupid friend back."

I remember him. He was the Amari hunter Peter and I saw at the mall before we kissed. He must be a part of the Grienzi. *What should I do? Act dumb? Challenge him?*

"Kiara, what is he talking about?" Clara's lip quivers; she stands as still as stone.

"Oh, you haven't told her? Well, let me break the news." His sarcastic tone lights a fire within me. "Your friend here is a part of the Amari. She has enhanced abilities and can beat the crap out of you. She's probably just being friends with you out of pity because she has so many cooler friends with special abilities." A smirk slides across his face.

"Is that true?" Clara's eyes look pleading, almost helpless. The man's words and the gun pointed at her head bring tears to her eyes.

"I am Amari, but I would never leave you. You are the best friend I could ever ask for."

"Aw. This is sweet and all, but I must get back to business. I'm going to take your friend here hostage and hold her for ransom."

"Not if I have anything to do with it." I reach into my waistband. Nowadays, I always keep a gun there. What? It's not there. My gun's not there. Where did it go?

"Looking for your gun? I had someone run into you earlier. Remember? Yeah, he took your gun. Really smart, right?" I remember. A young man ran into me and grabbed my waist. I didn't think much of it at the time. Now, it might cost me the life of my best friend.

Without another thought, I raise my fists to my face and storm towards him. However, I stop dead in my tracks when he loads the gun. "I wouldn't take another step. Your friend is one of ten civilians that will be captured today. Along with them, Vice President William Jones will be held for ransom. We want to meet with the Amari leader and the president alone. You have one week before we start shooting the hostages. When you agree, contact us on this phone." He tosses me a flip phone. "No cops, no weapons. They have to be alone, or it will get bloody. If you don't agree by the end of the week, your little friend here will be the first to die."

He walks backward out of the store and hides the gun behind Clara's back. Her lip is trembling, and tears stream down her face. I can't move. I don't know what to do. My best friend was just captured.

After five minutes of staring in shock, I stumble back to my car. The police were alerted about the hostage situation, but they were too late. There was nothing they could do.

Trying to keep it together, I drive to Luke's house and run into the guest room. I slam the door and sit down on the floor. Tears start pouring from my eyes. I look down at the flip phone, turning it over in my hands.

A few minutes later, I hear a knock at the door. "Kiara, are you okay?" It's Luke. I really don't want to talk right now, especially about Clara.

"No." I try to talk loudly, but my voice comes out in a whisper. Luke walks in and sits down next to me. He gently grabs my hand, and we sit in silence for a few minutes. I cry silently, letting the tears run down my face.

"Do you want to talk about it?"

"Not really, but I will." I look at the phone and place it on the ground. "I went shopping with Clara today. The Amari hunter that we saw on our last mission came to the mall and took Clara hostage. The Grienzi now have ten civilian hostages along with the vice president, and they want to meet the president and the leader of the Amari alone. They left this phone with me for when we contact them. We have a week before they start shooting the civilians." A sob escapes my mouth. "And now, my best friend is as good as dead, and I can't do anything about it."

"Hey, look at me." I lift my eyes to his. His face looks blurry from my tears. "Clara is going to be all right. We are going to get her back safely. I will not let what happened to my best friend happen to yours."

"I hope you're right. I just need to get my mind off of it right now."

"Well, that might not happen because we have to alert the rest of the Amari."

Dread starts building up inside of me. If we alert them, then that means I have to re-explain this whole story to a large crowd of people. I don't want to relive those moments, relive that helpless feeling. "I can't do it, Luke."

"Kiara, I know it hurts. Believe me, I know exactly how you feel. But this will be the only way that we can ensure her safety."

"Can we at least wait until tomorrow? I need a day to prepare."

"Sure, as long as we tell them first thing in the morning."

My attempt at a smile fails. "Thanks."

I cry myself to sleep that night. What would I do without Clara? My lifelong best friend is gone. I need to get her back. I must get her back. I will get her back.

CHAPTER 23

THE BUZZ OF my bracelet wakes me up from a deep sleep. I am not in the mood to tell a bunch of strangers about my personal loss, but what choice do I have? Reluctantly, I get up and hop in the car. Luke then drives me to the facility. When we arrive, Luke guides me to the door, placing his hand on the small of my back. His presence gives me a sense of peace.

Like last time, all the Amari are already grouped in the middle of the room, waiting for me to explain the incident. When Greg sees us, he walks up to me and whispers, "Luke briefed me on the incident, and I'm so sorry. If it's not too much to ask, we would all benefit if you were the one to explain it to the group instead of Luke because you witnessed the event first-hand."

"Okay." I turn to the group, keeping a straight face. "Yesterday, at the mall, Clara was kidnapped by an Amari hunter." My face gets hot. "Her, along with the vice president and nine other civilians, are being held captive right now by the Grienzi." I feel all eyes on me. "They want to meet the president and the leader of the Amari alone. We have one week to contact them using this phone, or they will start killing the hostages." I hold up the flip phone as my eyes start to water. *Don't cry, Kiara. Don't cry.* "That's all."

The room bursts into chaos. Luke pulls me to the side of the room.

"You're so brave, you know?"

I wipe my eyes and nod. "Thanks, Luke. Now, I'm going to go get my stitches out. Are you coming?" I need to take my mind off of Clara.

"Of course, I'm coming." Luke grabs my hand, and we walk over to the medics.

A doctor greets us, saying, "Welcome back, Kiara. How's your leg?"

"Good. I think it's healed." My voice is still shaky, but I try to keep it steady. "Can the stitches come out today?"

"Let's see. Can you please sit on that table?" I sit on the metal table that he gestures towards. Once I am seated, he looks at the scar and prods it with his fingers. "Yes, the stitches can come out today. Is now a suitable time?"

"I have nothing better to do, so yes."

"Okay, let me go get some scissors." A few moments later, the doctor comes back with surgical scissors and tells me to prop my leg up on the table. He carefully clips each stitch, pulling them out slowly. All I feel is a slight, tugging feeling. "You're all good. Just keep it clean and make sure it doesn't get infected."

"Thank you, doctor." I hop off the table and grab Luke's hand. All I want to do right now is go home. I need to cry, to feel Clara's loss, to allow myself to accept the fact that she is gone. As we reach the door to the facility, Greg beckons us over to a table surrounded by Amari members. So much for going home early.

"We want you and Luke to review our plan. Since you have witnessed the past few events, we would love your opinion. Plus, Luke is one of the strongest Amari here."

By this point, I am exhausted and just want to lie down, but this is the fastest way to get Clara back. "Sure, we'll look over it."

They show us the plan. Ten of the strongest Amari will secretly accompany Greg and the president to the meeting. When they get a clear shot, they will shoot the leader. I look at the list of Amari. Luke and I are both on the list. "So, if we get a clear shot, we fire. Why not shoot her legs so she is alive but she can't get away?"

"That's a good point. We will change that. Thank you."

"And, why not put all of the Amari into action? If we know the Grienzi are there, we will need all of the help we can get. Plus, there is no way the Grienzi are coming alone either."

"That's a great point." Greg scribbles some notes on the paper before looking back up. "Last thing, can we have the flip phone just so we can keep tabs on the Grienzi?"

"Actually, I thought I would keep it so you would notify us every time you want to contact them." There is no way I am going to let them keep the only means of communication to a terrorist group that has innocent civilians taken hostage, one of them being my best friend. Without another word to them, I leave with Luke. Was that a little rude? Maybe. Did they have good intentions? Most likely. However, my best friend was just kidnapped, and they expect me to give them the closest tie I have to her right now. There is no way that is happening.

As we walk across the street, Luke asks me, "Do you want to go on a date?"

"No offense, Luke, but now is not the time."

"Now is the perfect time. You need to take your mind off of Clara and the Grienzi, and I want alone time with you."

I just shrug my shoulders. "If you insist. What do you have in mind?"

"I was thinking of having a picnic at the park. There is already food in my car; I packed it this morning."

"You knew I would say yes?"

"I knew I could convince you." A smile spreads across his face as he grabs my hand. Luke opens the car door for me and lets me climb in. He then drives us to the nearest park and unpacks the picnic items.

We take a seat in an open, grassy area. The sun washes over my skin, and a slight breeze rustles the trees. I cherish this relaxing moment, knowing there won't be another for a while. Luke, however, does not share this peaceful feeling. His face is bunched together, deep in thought. "A penny for your thoughts?"

"What?" Startled, Luke looks over at me.

"You look worried. What are you thinking about?"

"Just about the Grienzi and the hostages."

I grab Luke's hand and brush my thumb over the top of it. "Luke, we're on a picnic in the middle of nature. So, stop worrying and just enjoy being in the moment. After all, it was your idea to take our minds off of everything."

Luke grins as he grabs a sandwich. "Okay, I'm sorry. I'll just enjoy being on a date with my beautiful girlfriend."

We both smile and continue eating. "You know, this is only our second date."

"Don't blame me, Kiara. Crime fighting takes a lot of time out of one's schedule."

I grin into my next bite and lean over to kiss him on the cheek. "Well, I'm honored that I get to fight crime by your side."

CH/\PTER 24

WE GATHER IN the Amari training facility. They called us today because there is a lead on where all the hostages are being held. There are two days left before the end of the week, two days before innocent civilians start dying.

"The Grienzi have hidden the hostages at the airport. We are going to join the Amari from neighboring cities to liberate them tonight. If you come in contact with any of the Grienzi at any point in time, shoot them. We will leave in thirty minutes. Go get ready." Mr. Davenport walks up to me and Luke. "Call the last dialed number on the flip phone. We need to tell the Grienzi we will meet them tonight."

I dial the number. A feminine voice answers the phone. "The Amari, I presume?"

Greg motions for Luke and me to be silent. Only he and the

president are supposedly meeting the Grienzi, so we can't be a part of this conversation. "Yes. Who is this?"

"The leader of the Grienzi."

"We're coming tonight."

"That's perfect. We'll be waiting at the airport. Come to the runway that is not being used; there is less chance of being run over by a plane. There are no cops, no weapons, just you and the president. See you then." She hangs up before Greg can get another word in.

As Greg leaves, my parents walk up to us. "You are going to do great, honey. We love you so much. Please stay with Luke, and don't get hurt." My mom has a worried look on her face.

"I love y'all so much. I'll come back. Don't worry." I run into their arms and hug them. Who knows? This could be the last time I ever see my parents.

"We'll be waiting," my dad whispers into my hair. "I love you."

I look into their eyes and try to reassure them. My manufactured smile does not ease their concern. After one more hug, I walk away with Luke to the weapons station so that my parents don't see the fear in my eyes. Focusing my mind on the upcoming mission, I grab an AR-15 and sling it across my back. Everyone is silent, except for the occasional murmur of the leaders. I join Frank, Luke, and the rest of our group by the entrance to the facility. "Time to go?"

Luke answers me with a silent nod.

We load up the trucks and head out. Greg and the president's look-alike are in the first car. There would have been no way the real president would risk his life for this. He is far too important, and the country needs him.

When we arrive at the back entrance of the airport, three different Amari groups come to welcome us. They are all from neighboring cities.

"Listen up! We will split up by cities." Greg stands in the middle. He is sweating profusely, and his hands are shaking, but he tries to maintain a calm stature. How would I feel if I were meeting people who wanted to kill me? "My group will face them head-on. Every other group will try to surround them. Get orders from your leaders. We will leave in 15 minutes."

I grab Luke's hand; I don't want to be separated from him. As previously instructed, the physically enhanced Amari from our city gather around Greg. "Okay, listen up! We will be facing the Grienzi head-on. Shoot on sight. Have no fear. Try to keep the leader alive. Disable her, but do not kill her. She will be brought in for questioning later."

He pauses for a second, collecting his thoughts. "We will make rows based on our prior groups. Luke's group will be in the front row. George's group will be in the second row. Diana's group will follow up in the rear. Does everybody understand? Greg receives murmurs and nods in response.

Hundreds of thoughts immediately flood my head. I am on the front line. I will face the Grienzi head-on. What if I see Clara? Will I get shot? How about killed? Will I ever see my parents again? What if Luke gets hurt?

Fifteen dreadful minutes pass. We wait in silence for the signal to head out. During this time, I try to clear my head. Fear builds up inside of me, but I try to push it aside.

Greg finally gives us the signal. The Amari from our city follow Greg and the president's look-alike onto the runway. It is dark outside, so we can barely see each other. I'm grateful for the darkness. It means no one can see me shaking, and the Grienzi can't tell that we didn't bring the real president. The darkness also conceals the Amari scattered around the runway, ready to shoot on command.

"Welcome, Mr. President. Welcome, Greg. How was your drive over here?"

"Cut the crap. We're here to negotiate." Greg's voice is stern. I can't make out who is talking, but I think it is the leader of the Grienzi I saw during the 2:00 a.m. meeting. She has the same feminine voice and rigid posture.

"Someone is fussy. Did you come alone?" She sounds playful, like she isn't taking this seriously.

"Do I look like I'm alone?" Greg doesn't wait for an answer. "Yes. It's just me and the president."

"I didn't mean to inconvenience you, Greg. Or you, Mr. President, with all of the important things happening in the world right now. To be honest, I just need to negotiate a few things."

"That's good because we are here to negotiate, too." The fake president is identical to the actual president, except that his voice is a bit deeper. I hope they don't notice.

"Let me get to the point. You can have your insignificant little citizens if you remove all U.S. troops from European countries. I want the United States to have nothing to do with that side of the world."

"That's a big request coming from such a small terrorist group," Greg says. "Why would you want that?"

"You think we are small? We would have taken over Europe if it hadn't been for the U.S. and your troops. Once you remove them, the Grienzi can conquer Europe and eventually the world."

"And why would you tell us your plan?"

"I don't care who knows it. If you don't agree right now, civilians will continue to die. I know how to hit the United States where it hurts. I already have orders being sent to capture 100 civilians from each state after this meeting. You think you are in control, but you're not. I can have 5,000 citizens dead tomorrow with just one phone call."

"I'm sorry, but we do not negotiate with terrorists."

"Tell that to her." She motions into the darkness. A short man brings forth a shaking girl. When I look closer, I see that it is the man who captured Clara. He is holding Clara by the neck, pointing a loaded gun at her head. I clamp my hand to my mouth to stifle a groan. Tears stream down her face, and bruises dot her face and arms.

Luke, who is a few feet from me, reaches out and grabs my hand. He holds it for a few seconds before dropping it again. Tears well up in my eyes. I can't stop myself from shaking at the thought of my best friend being beaten and tortured.

"Go on. Tell her she will die because you won't remove your troops."

Clara shakes her head. "I don't want to die," she whimpers in between sobs.

"You won't die, young lady. We will figure something out," the President says.

"Figure something out? There's nothing to figure out. I've given you my terms. Accept them, and the hostages will be freed. Deny them, and the hostages, along with many more civilians, will die."

Turning towards the president, Greg mutters a few words. Before we left for this mission, Greg told all the Amari to attack when he agreed to the terms and said, "We will accept your offer." After a few moments of this so-called deliberation, Greg turns back to the leader. Everyone around me raises their guns and steadies themselves. We all know what's about to come. Following suit, I wipe the tears from my face and shoulder my gun. I line the sights up with the leader.

Greg solemnly says, "We will accept your offer." Gunshots go off everywhere. The leader falls to the ground, but the man holding Clara shuffles back into the darkness. "Go! Go! Find them!" Greg shouts.

The leader writhes in pain on the ground; she has three bullet holes in her body. Greg quickly slaps cuffs on her and then calls an ambulance. Although she is a criminal, the U.S. would rather have her alive in jail than possibly dead and on the loose.

Once the leader is secured, I follow the man who was holding Clara. All around me, guns are being fired. Grienzi members from behind the planes flood the runway; the Grienzi leader didn't come alone either. The Amari split up, trying to neutralize all of the Grienzi.

The noise from the screams and the gunshots reverberates off of the unused planes, carrying endlessly across the runways. Determined to rescue Clara, I ignore this sudden chaos and follow the man who was holding my friend.

Luke runs at my heels. "I assume you're going to find Clara."

"You don't have to come if you don't want to, Luke." While I want Luke by my side, I don't want him to feel obligated to risk his life for me.

Smiling, Luke says, "I'd rather be with you." A warm feeling swells in my chest, but it doesn't last long. My ears ring from the gunshots. It smells like gunpowder, and fog rises from the ground.

Luke and I sneak around a few planes. The runway we met on has been under construction for several months, so no planes are actively using it. That means there are many unused planes and trucks to hide behind. Where could they be?

Screams coming from the entrance to the terminal draw my attention. We silently creep into the terminal, following the screams. Every so often, I hear a "Shut up" followed by a thud and a grunt. My heart breaks at the sound of my best friend being beaten.

Eventually, the footsteps and screams stop; we have reached Gate 23. Luke and I silently creep behind a corner. I peer around and see eleven people sitting side-by-side in the boarding area. Some are silently crying, others are staring vacantly into space, and a few are shaking violently.

Turning to Luke, I whisper, "I'll sneak around and distract the guard. Free the hostages and get them out of here."

"Kiara, I can't let you do this. Let me fight him." His eyes search mine, desperately looking for something deep inside me. Hope, maybe, or fear. Luke doesn't want me risking my life while he goes unharmed.

"I need to do this. That man broke me when he took Clara; this is my way to finally strike back at him. Just make sure the hostages are safe. I'll try to distract him so he doesn't shoot at you."

Luke meets my eyes and grabs my face, firmly pressing his lips to mine. Giving me one last hug, he reluctantly backs away and lifts his gun to his shoulder. "I'll wait until you lure him away." Luke pauses for a second. "And no matter what, don't get hurt. I'm coming back for you when everyone is safe. I can't lose you, too."

CH△PTER 25

BEFORE I CAN back down, I push myself out into the middle of the hall. "Hey!"

"What are you doing here?" His deep, rough voice brings back a vivid memory from when he captured Clara.

"What do you think? I'm going to knock you out, and then I'll free the hostages." Hopefully, this man is narcissistic; otherwise, he might not take the bait. "I could beat you up easily."

"You want to bet, little girl?"

"Yeah. If I win, then you must free the hostages. If you win, then you can keep the hostages and have me as well." My eyes catch Clara's. Her tear-streaked face is begging me to leave her and get somewhere safe, but I can't do that. I can't leave her.

The man pauses for a few seconds, debating whether this is a good idea. "Okay, deal." He runs at me without saying another word, forcing me to stutter back a few steps. While I'm trying to be brave, fear floods my mind as this fully grown man with a loaded gun runs towards me. Throwing his gun to the floor, he lunges at me. Out of the corner of my eye, I see Luke running toward the hostages.

I try to dodge his flying body, but he manages to punch me in the face. He must be really strong because that punch really hurt. Normal punches don't hurt Amari like that. Ignoring my throbbing jaw, I block a punch and kick him in the stomach. He stumbles back, but recoils twice as hard.

"Is that all you got?" He lunges at me, and we both tumble to the floor. I elbow him in the head, and he punches me in the ribs. With blood trickling down his face, he punches me twice in the jaw. That's going to hurt later. In an effort to disable him momentarily, I pull my knee into his groin. Showing no reaction to the pain, he grabs my arm and twists it at an angle it should not bend. A scream of pain and frustration escapes my mouth. I sweep my leg under his, knocking him from his feet. Before he can get back up, I straddle him and punch him in the face. After the third punch, he grabs my fist and crushes it. He pushes me off of him and stands up straight.

As I stumble to my feet, I glance at the gate where the hostages were. I see Luke running towards the exit with the rest of them. A sense of relief washes over me; they are safe. "Are you hurt, little girl?" he hisses at me, drawing my attention back to him.

"Shut up. I'm not finished with you." My side aches, and my jaw throbs.

"Suit yourself. It's your funeral, not mine."

With a twisted smirk on his face, he walks towards me and draws his fist back. Before he can punch me, I kick him square in the chest, causing him to fall to the floor. I feel a burst of energy. I jump on top of him and start punching every inch of his body. His face bleeds out around his right eye and upper lip. My knuckles pound his face. I feel alive; I will win. I punch his nose and hear a crack. He groans in pain and throws me off of him. Feeling triumphant, I stand up and pull my fists to my face. "Still think I'm a little girl?"

Rubbing the blood from his eyes, he says, "I'm done with this. Like I said, it's your funeral." He reaches down to the floor and grabs his gun. He lifts it to his face and cocks it. My face goes slack; I forgot he had a gun. Where is mine? Too late. He fires.

It's slow motion. I watch the bullet leave the barrel. I can't move in time. It hits my left shoulder, inches from my heart. I look up at him as a smile stretches across the man's bloodied face. I see Luke at the end of the hallway, running toward us, a look of distress replacing his usually calm demeanor. Luke fires two bullets into my opponent's chest.

I fall to the floor, my shoulder throbbing. Pain travels through my body like liquid fire.

"Kiara!" I barely hear him over the pounding in my ears. Luke rushes over to me. My vision is hazy. He places his hand on my head just as the medics arrive. Black spots dot the edges of my vision. Who knew I could be in this much pain?

The medics place me on a stretcher and carry me to the ambulance. Every shift of the stretcher sends searing pain through my body. Luke jogs beside me, squeezing my hand. I hear wailing noises and muffled talk. I can make out a few words such as 'will make her delusional' and 'will help ease the pain.' *What are they injecting into my body?*

They lift me into the van and put something over my mouth. A medic pushes me up to a sitting position and puts both hands on either side of my wound. He squeezes the wound, applying intense pressure that makes me tremble.

Pain travels through my shoulder, setting every inch on fire. I let out a groan, but my body is screaming. The medicine in the tube that is placed over my mouth makes me feel drowsy. I can't see straight. My head is splitting, but the pain won't go away. When will it stop?

We reach the hospital, and I am wheeled into a surgery room. People in blue outfits rush around me. My heart is pounding in my ears. A man with a surgical mask leans over me, placing something over my mouth and nose.

Panic rises in me. *What is he giving me?* My shoulder is throbbing. I am drowsy from the earlier medicine, but the pain still hasn't subsided. All I want right now is sleep. I feel a few pinches near the bullet wound. What if they injected me with more liquid fire?

My world goes black as my body succumbs to the pain.

CHAPTER 26

I BLINK A COUPLE of times as my eyes adjust to the bright lights. My shoulder throbs. I notice that it is wrapped in blood-stained gauze. An IV is injected into my right arm, and I am in a hospital bed.

After a few moments, I tilt my head to the right. "Luke," I croak. Luke is sitting in a blue chair next to my bed. His eyebrows are wrinkled, and his jaw is tightly clenched.

When Luke hears me, he immediately stands up and rushes to my side. "Kiara, how are you feeling?"

I smile and laugh but quickly stop. The sudden movement pains my shoulder. "I'm okay right now. What happened?" My voice sounds hoarse, and it is barely audible over the humming of the machines around me.

"You were shot in your left shoulder at the airport. I called the medics, and you went directly into surgery. They removed the bullet successfully." His eyes are swollen, and tears streak his face. Luke only cries when he is extremely worried. "You have a broken rib, not to mention all of the other bruises on your face and side."

"Now you can say your girlfriend has been shot twice." My delusional joke has no effect on him. His face remains solemn.

"This is all my fault. I should have faced him, not you."

"Luke, it's not your fault. It was my score to settle, and I was too foolish to think I could win without injuring myself."

He sighs and grabs my hand. "Your parents are here, but they said they wanted me to be the first person you would see when you woke up."

"Can I see them?"

"Of course."

"And Luke, I love you. Don't worry, okay?"

Luke smiles at me and walks away without another word. Seconds later, my parents enter the room with Jacob at their heels.

"Kiara, how are you?" My mom rushes to my side and grabs my hand. My dad rushes to the other side of my bed, grabbing my other hand.

"I'm good, Mom. How are you two?"

"We're fine," my dad says. "Do you need anything?"

"No, I am fine."

"You are so brave, you know that?" Mom bends over to kiss my forehead. Both of them have watery eyes and tissues stuffed in their pockets. I never realized just how many people cared for me, but it is clearly evident by their tear-streaked faces and tissue-stuffed pockets.

Jacob walks up to me; even his eyes are swollen. "You don't look too good, Jacob."

"You don't look too good, either, Kiara." He smiles. "I'm glad you're okay. I don't know what I would do without you."

"That's very sweet of you. I love you, too, Jacob."

Then, I remember the one reason I went after that gruff man in the first place: Clara. "Is Clara safe?"

"Yes, she is. She's here. All seven of us have spent every hour here waiting for you."

"Seven?"

"Yes. Alex and Frank are here, too."

"Really?" A feeling of peace washes over me as I realize the magnitude of my friends' love for me.

"Do you want to see Clara?"

"Yes." They both kiss my hand and walk away. Before they leave, I whisper, "I love y'all."

"We love you, too." My parents walk out of the room as Clara walks in.

"Clara," I croak as loud as I can.

Clara rushes over to me and kneels by my bed. "Don't waste energy on raising your voice." She is smiling, but her eyes are red and puffy from crying.

"How are you? Did you get out all right? I told Luke to bring you and the rest of the hostages to safety." Her face still shows signs of bruising.

"I'm not the one with the bullet wound, but if you have to know, I am fine." Clara grabs my hand. "I heard you will be out in three weeks."

"You forgot; I am Amari. That means I'll be out in a week or two."

"So, what the man said was true. You are an Amari." She frowns. If that is true, she probably thinks the other part is true: the part where I have better Amari friends.

"I am Amari, but you are still my best friend." I look her dead in the eyes. "I promise."

Her face lightens, and her easy smile returns. "That's good because you are my best friend, too." She gives me a big hug, careful to avoid my left shoulder. "So, what are we going to do for the next couple of weeks?"

"Talk about Alex."

Clara blushes but then smiles and says, "Only if we can talk about Luke."

"Deal."

Mom, Dad, and Luke enter the room again, followed by Frank, Alex, and Jacob. Frank and Alex run up to me with excited faces.

"Kiara!"

"Hi, Alex. Hi, Frank." A smile stretches across my face. These are my people. I love them, and they all care about me.

"So, you're an Amari? Frank told me all about it," Alex says.

"Yes, I'm an Amari."

"We're still friends, right? I mean, if you have other Amari friends, that's cool."

"Alex, you all are my friends." He smiles.

Everyone pulls up a chair and sits around my bed. Clara squeezes in next to me on my hospital bed while my mom and dad sit on a couch in the corner, reading a magazine. I can tell they are eavesdropping on our conversation, but I don't mind.

"So, when did you two start dating?" Alex points at Luke and me. I smile and turn to Luke, letting him answer the question.

"Around the beginning of Strength training, right after our first fight. Better yet, when did you two start dating?" Luke points to Clara and Alex.

"About halfway through Strength training."

"I knew it," Luke mutters.

Everyone turns to Luke. "What?" I demand.

"Being an instructor means you notice the little things, like holding hands when a couple leaves or quick glances between each other. I knew from around the start of training that y'all liked each other."

"No way." Clara crosses her arms and playfully stares Luke down. "We were barely friends."

"For one, Clara basically stared at Alex all of the time. And when Clara wasn't staring, Alex couldn't keep his eyes off of her. It was so hard to watch. About halfway through training, Frank would leave early with Sarah, and Kiara would stay behind for me, so you two were always alone. That meant y'all could hold hands when y'all left."

"You've put a lot of thought into this, haven't you?" Alex says playfully.

"How did you even do that?" Jacob asks, shocked like everyone else.

"I pay careful attention to details. Plus, y'all are my girlfriend's best friends."

"That's crazy. You could be a detective or something," Frank says incredulously.

Clara whispers into my ear, "You picked wisely."

A grin spreads across my face. "I know. Luke is the best boyfriend."

While Mom and Dad read magazines and books, we continue talking about many things, from our summer to our favorite foods to our new jobs.

After a few weeks of resting in bed, the doctor releases me from the hospital. According to him, I can expect a few months of physical therapy, depending on the speed of my arm's recovery.

My parents give me a big hug and promise to visit in the next few days. Luke then drives me to his house. When we get home, I head straight to bed. Before I can drift asleep, Luke says, "I want to take you somewhere tonight. Are you up for it?"

Grinning, I respond, "Am I up for a date night with my boyfriend? Always."

"Great. I'm going to the store to get painkillers. I'll be back around 5:30, so we can leave at 6:00 tonight."

"Sounds great. See you soon." Before I can finish the sentence, I am fast asleep.

When Luke returns from the store, he gently wakes me up from my nap. He patiently waits for me to get dressed, helping when necessary. Once we are both ready, Luke drives us to the same hotel where we had our first date.

Luke looks over at me and says, "Don't worry. I want to take you to the top of the building."

Smiling, I remember back to our first date. We have grown in so many ways since that night, and I am so grateful for all of the memories I have shared with Luke.

We take an elevator to the hotel's roof, enjoying each other's company on the way up. Once we reach the top, we walk over to the edge. The gentle breeze tousles my hair. Luke grabs my hand, rubbing it with his thumb.

The view is breathtaking. Colorful lights of red, blue, and yellow fill the sky. Each building has a colorful silhouette, outlined in bright flashing lights or softer glows. Trees are wrapped in vibrant colors. The beautiful landscape is overwhelming and takes my breath away. It reminds me of how small we are in this massive world.

I turn to Luke in this moment of awe, noticing the playful grin on his face. "What is it, Luke?"

Luke brings his eyes to mine, staring deep into my soul. "I just can't believe how far we have come."

"What do you mean?"

"A couple of months ago, we were total strangers. You beat me up in the ring, and I fell for you. I fell in love with your determination and those eyes that shine like diamonds. We have laughed together, cried together, and fought together. Now, after defeating a terrorist group, we are sitting at the top of a building overlooking one of the most beautiful sights in the city."

"Well, I wouldn't have it any other way." A contagious grin spreads across my face.

"Neither would I." With that, he presses his lips to mine. Luke wraps his arms around my waist, pulling me closer to him. As I wrap my arm around his neck, he gently trails his fingers along the small of my back.

This is how it should be. My friends and family are safe; I am with the ones I love. While wrapped in Luke's arms and sharing this space with him, a sense of peace washes over me. We are safe. We are together. We are family.

"I love you, Luke."

"I love you, too, Kiara."

Epilogue: 1 year later

"KIARA, ARE YOU ready? We are going to be late!" Luke knocks on my door as he slides on his other shoe.

After I tie my shoelaces, I open the door and find him standing with his arms crossed. "What?"

"You said you were ready ten minutes ago. Now, we're going to be the last ones to arrive at lunch."

"Not on my watch." Snatching the keys from his hands, I give him a playful smirk. Luke closes the door behind me, shaking his head as a grin engulfs his face.

Fifteen minutes pass as I speed down the highway. When we get to the restaurant, I find Clara sitting at a table outside with Alex, Frank, and Lora. It is under a big oak tree, guarding us from the brutal summer heat.

"Kiara! Over here!" With a big smile on her face, Clara beckons us over. "What took y'all so long? I'm starving."

"Kiara decided to take an extra long time to get ready." Luke glances over at me, smirking as I elbow him in the ribs.

"We're here now. Did we miss anything?" I say, sitting down next to Clara. Luke sits down across from me.

"Frank was just telling us about this new workout trainer who is really quite cute." Lora laughs as Frank blushes. "What? Those were your exact words."

"Yeah, yeah, get the jokes out now. Her name is Grace, and she has blonde hair and these vibrant blue eyes."

"Almost like Sarah, huh?" Alex grins as he takes a sip of water. Frank punches his arm, making Alex spill water down his shirt.

"Y'all know I ended that a long time ago."

"We know, Frank. Alex is just joking." Clara hides her giggle, gently nudging Alex. Then, changing the subject, she asks, "Lora, have you found anyone yet?"

"Actually, there's this guy that I have been talking to recently. Nothing major yet, but he is very handsome and one of the nicest guys I have met."

Luke's head swivels toward her. "Who is he, and why have I not heard about him?"

"Calm down, Luke. No need to go into overprotective brother mode."

"I'm not." Luke tries to ease his shoulders as he folds his hands in his lap. "All I would like to know is his name. Maybe his address as well."

"As much as y'all want to know, his name will be a secret until I figure out if we are going to be more than friends or not."

Attempting to put on a serious face, I say, "Despite how badly we want to know this mystery man, I guess we can respect your decision. Right, guys?" Everyone reluctantly agrees to let Lora keep her secrets.

Once the waiter walks over to our table, we each take turns ordering food. After I order, I stare off into space, waiting for the rest of my friends. I start fidgeting with the rings on my fingers. Luke and I asked everyone here for a fun lunch, but in reality we have some big news to tell them. But when should I slip it into the conversation?

"Kiara, did you hear Paul got demoted?" Drawn from my thoughts, I look over at Alex.

"What? Is that even possible?"

Frank continues eagerly, "Yeah. He is such a bad teacher that he is stuck with the little kids now. Apparently, the summer we spent training last year meant nothing because he is, and I quote, 'underqualified' and 'disregards any progress made.' His boss was so mad because Paul was supposed to be the second best in our section, but he ended up being a stuck-up teenager who only cares about himself. Paul went from training top fighters to five-year-olds."

Laughing hysterically, Frank slaps his thigh. Alex cracks up next to him, and I can't help but laugh, too. While I feel bad for all the pressure from his parents, Paul deserved to be humbled.

"I bet Paul didn't see that coming," Clara chips in. Her smile shows she is content to know that karma has finally caught up with him.

"Never really liked that kid. Paul, is that his name? He acted as if he was better than everyone else in the room, even the instructors." A look of annoyance crosses Lora's face as she continues. "Even when I was teaching, he would look at me as if I was stupid."

"Those were the good days," Luke adds, glancing over at me. "When we were your superiors." He proudly grins as we give him funny looks. "I remember when Clara and Alex started dating. Man, that was painful to watch." Luke's smile intensifies as Alex's face turns an even brighter shade of red.

Frank slides in, saying, "Alex used to come back to the dorms in another world. Before some of your dates, he would tell me about how nervous he was to hold your hand, Clara."

"Frank! I would appreciate it if we don't rehash the awkward phases of our relationship." Alex puts his head in his hands to hide his embarrassment. Frank, on the other hand, can't contain his laughter.

"And remember how you and Luke were dating too!" Clara grins as she recalls those days. "I was shocked when I found out about you two."

"Your face when you saw us kiss for the first time was so funny. You couldn't keep your mouth closed." Everyone at the table starts laughing now. Pure joy overwhelms me as I sit here with my friends. This is how life should always be.

After our food comes, we eat and continue talking. However, a lingering thought nags at the back of my head: we need to tell them. When is the right time, though?

"So, Luke, how has it been sharing a house with Kiara? I know it's convenient being close to the training facility and all, but is it awkward?"

"Not really. We each have our own rooms, and since our jobs are similar, we usually see each other throughout the day. Plus, it is really nice to come home and hang out with your best friend."

Now's the time; I just need to tell them. Clasping my hands in my lap, I look over at Luke. He nods his head, giving me an understood blessing that it is time.

"So, you all know we organized the lunch as a little hangout, but we actually have some big news to tell y'all."

"What is it?" Clara looks me dead in the eyes, trying to decipher what I am about to say.

I pause, letting the suspense build in the air. "C'mon. Just tell us, Kiara." Frank looks impatient as he awaits our news.

With a final glance at Luke, I look at our friends. A big grin spreads across my face as I say, "Luke and I are getting married!"

About the Author

Jocelyn Loftus is a young woman dedicated to her passion for writing. She loves her family and friends and finds joy in being active outdoors. When she was young, she loved captivating books and would spend hours reading in a cozy spot. Since then, her love for reading and writing has grown immensely.

Jocelyn embarked on writing Amari when she was just 14 years old. Inspired by authors like Veronica Roth, who increased her love of literature, she incorporated the importance of family and friends into this exciting novel. She feels grateful for the journey this book has taken her on, and she hopes it will continue for many years.

The main character, Kiara, embodies the Bible verses in Philippians 2:3-4. Through this book, Jocelyn hopes to spread God's Word through each of her characters. Someone's physical and eternal life might be saved through true love and humility towards others.

www.ingramcontent.com/pod-product-compliance
Lightning Source LLC
Chambersburg PA
CBHW071330250626
47159CB00004B/1549